What Teens Are Saying About
DIARY OF A TEENAGE GIRL SERIES...

"These books have taken over my bookshelf. Every time I read another one I laugh, I cry, and I understand how God can use people to change so many situations."

"From the first entry of *Becoming Me* by Caitlin O'Conner to her last entry in *I Do*, I feel amazed by her strong faith and commitment to God. She gives me—and all the young people my age—a new hope and encourages us to lean on God and continue to have a strong faith."

"I just finished the third Caitlin book, and it made me feel close to God and hopeful for the future! In the past year, I've read many books, all of which supported sex before marriage...and then I found the Diary of a Teenage Girl series. I really appreciate that it is Christian and discourages sex before marriage. I am going to tell all of my friends about your books!"

"Wow, I can't get over how wonderful your books are—they are such an inspiration! I have always gone to church with my family, and I've known about God but never really took Him seriously. I've learned so many things from the Diary series and HAVE ASKED GOD INTO MY HEART!"

"I've read all the Chloe books—and they're great! It's interesting to see the changes in Chloe. Some of the trials she went through helped me learn about myself and what to do in similar circumstances, and I'm truly grateful for that and pray that God will continue to bless others through your work."

"I am currently reading *Becoming Me*. I love this book so much! It showed me how I needed to work on my relationship with God. I absolutely love it. Keep up the great work."

Diary of a Teenage Girl

Kim Book No. 4

That Was Then...

a novel

MELODY CARLSON

MULTNOMAH
BOOKS

This is a work of fiction. The characters, incidents, and dialogues are products of the author's imagination and are not to be construed as real. Any resemblance to actual events or persons, living or dead, is entirely coincidental.

THAT WAS THEN...
published by Multnomah Books
and in association with the literary agency of Sara A. Fortenberry

International Standard Book Number: 1-59052-425-X

Cover design by Studiogearbox.com
Cover image by Haruka Demura/Getty Images

Published in the United States by WaterBrook Multnomah, an imprint of the Crown Publishing Group, a division of Random House Inc., New York.

Printed in the United States of America

For information:
MULTNOMAH BOOKS
12265 ORACLE BOULEVARD, SUITE 200
COLORADO SPRINGS, CO 80921

Library of Congress Cataloging-in-Publication Data
Carlson, Melody.
That was then-- / by Melody Carlson.
p. cm. -- (Diary of a teenage girl series. Kim ; bk. #4)
Summary: Kim faces many changes her senior year in high school, including Nat's hasty wedding, childbirth, and ultimate decision about the baby, the first holidays without her mother, new problems for cousin Maya, and a significant surprise from her past.
ISBN 1-59052-425-X
[1. Mothers and daughters--Fiction. 2. Pregnancy--Fiction. 3. Marriage--Fiction. 4. Christian life--Fiction. 5. Korean Americans--Fiction. 6. Advice columns--Fiction. 7. Diaries--Fiction.]
I. Title.
PZ7.C216637Tha 2006
[Fic]--dc22
2006000693

12 13 14 15 16—10 9 8 7 6 5 4

Books by Melody Carlson:

Piercing Proverbs

DIARY OF A TEENAGE GIRL SERIES

Caitlin O'Conner:

Becoming Me

It's My Life

Who I Am

On My Own

I Do!

Chloe Miller:

My Name Is Chloe

Sold Out

Road Trip

Face the Music

Kim Peterson:

Just Ask

Meant to Be

Falling Up

That Was Then…

TRUE COLOR SERIES

Dark Blue, color me lonely

Deep Green, color me jealous

Torch Red, color me torn

Pitch Black, color me lost

Burnt Orange, color me wasted

Fool's Gold, color me consumed

Blade Silver, color me scarred

Bitter Rose, color me broken

One

Monday, September 4

School starts tomorrow. My senior year. And although it's not something I advertise to my peers since it would permanently cast me as the class geek, I am glad. I look forward to the routine. I look forward to my classes and to seeing teachers again. I even look forward to the smell of floor cleaner, chalk dust, and books. Seriously, I actually like the smell of school. How lame is that?

I'm sure an even bigger reason that I want school to start has to do with Nat. I'm so sick of hearing her go on about how happy she and Ben and the baby are going to be...how beautiful their wedding's going to be...how God has truly blessed them in an unexpected way. And I can't let on to her how sickening this is to me. Or how I still think it's a great, big, fat mistake for two seventeen-year-olds to get married. Or how it's really hard playing the role of her best friend these days. No, I just have to smile and act like everything's peachy.

Yeah, right.

The only thing that keeps me from totally losing it is my relationship with God. Seriously, I feel like I'm starting to depend on Him for everything these days. And that's what gets me through. There's a Bible verse, 2 Corinthians 12:9, that says God gets glorified by our weaknesses because we have to lean on Him, and as a result, He gets to really shine in us. I think that's been my personal theme verse this past summer.

And I really have to kick this verse into gear on days like today. Here I was, thinking how I was just going to hang around and enjoy the last day before school starts. Maybe get a few things done at home, practice my violin, answer some letters in my Just Ask Jamie column, but then Nat calls up and insists we go shopping. And she doesn't mean back-to-school shopping. No, that would be too obvious, too simple. Nat wants me to go with her to look for her wedding dress and my maid of honor dress. What an honor!

And never mind that all the last-minute back-to-school shoppers are out in hordes, or that the parking lots are packed full, or that it's nearly 100 degrees out. We still have to go shopping.

"We can't keep putting this off," she tells me when she calls late this morning.

"Just for a week?"

"Fine," she says in an aggravated tone. "But just so

you know, I already invited Caitlin to join us today. If you don't want to come, well, I'll tell her you're too busy, and she and I will do it on our own."

I let out a long sigh. "I'll come."

"Great!" Now the tone of her voice is the old cheerful Nat again. "It'll be fun, Kim. Just the three of us."

"Your mom's not coming?"

"No, she has to work. She told me how much I can spend, which is going to be a serious challenge. But Caitlin said she's got some ideas."

So it's agreed. And although I try to be a good sport and I keep my smiley face on throughout most of the day, I am so ready for this to be over. After exhausting our options at the traditional mall, where all the wedding gowns are out of Nat's price range, we head on over to an outlet mall. And the final shop seems to show the most promise. At least when it comes to price tags.

Caitlin learned about this little discount shop when she was looking for her own wedding gown. Of course, as it turned out, her good friend Beanie Jacobs, who goes to this big New York design school, created a gown that was a perfect dream. Caitlin looked like a princess in it.

"How about this one for you, Kim?" Caitlin holds up an elegant green dress with some beadwork and an uneven hemline.

"But Nat wants me to wear orange," I remind her as I stand in front of the three-way mirror and frown at this burnt orange number I've got on that is so long the overly full skirt poufs out like a hot-air balloon around me.

Caitlin shakes her head. "Those orange and gold tones don't do a thing for your skin tones, Kim. I think I'll try to talk Natalie into a cool color."

"Cool's good for me," I say, not quite sure what she means by that, but willing to do anything that's an improvement over this sorry dress.

"What about this?" Nat says, as she finally emerges from the dressing room with the saleswoman right behind her. It's about the hundredth dress she's tried on today. And I have to say that her stamina (especially in light of being pregnant) is rather impressive.

Caitlin and I both stand back and study the cream-colored satiny dress as Natalie takes my spot in front of the big mirror.

"The sweetheart neckline looks very nice on her," the saleswoman points out. I wonder if this woman is getting low on patience yet. Or maybe it's just me. But I must agree that this dress does look quite nice.

"Not bad," I say to my best friend. The good news is that I actually mean it this time. "It's simple but elegant, and that style really seems to suit you, Nat." Not for the first time, I feel a small wave of envy for her height advantage. Seriously, that girl can wear anything. Well, at least when she's not enormously pregnant. We'll see how she looks a few months from now.

Nat pats the small rounded belly that's become a bit more obvious lately. "And the way the waistline is cut high like this sort of disguises the baby," she says. "Don't you think?"

"Is there room to get bigger?" Caitlin asks. "My aunt Steph warned me that the baby will really start to grow after the fifth month. She said to make sure you get a dress with a little room, just in case."

Nat checks the dress around her waistline. "I think it'll be okay. I mean, it's only three weeks till the wedding. You wouldn't think I could get too big in that short amount of time."

Caitlin shakes her head as she looks at the dress more closely. "I don't know, Nat. Just to be safe, you might want the next size up. Why don't you just try it and see?" Then she holds up the dress she's picked out for me. "Don't you think this mossy green would be pretty on Kim?"

Nat frowns. "I wanted to have fall colors." Then she turns and really looks at me in this poufy orange number and actually starts laughing. "You look like the Great Pumpkin, Kim!"

"Thanks a lot."

Now she studies me for a moment. "Yeah, maybe that color's not so good on you, Kim. Go ahead and try on some green ones. Just make sure they're not springy-looking greens, Caitlin."

"This earthy green would still look great with the fall-colored flowers you picked out," Caitlin tells her. "In fact, the bridesmaid bouquet will probably stand out even better against this."

"Caitlin's grandmother-in-law is helping us with the flowers," Nat tells me.

Okay, I've already heard this like six times already. "That's nice," I say with my pasted-on smile.

"Shall I get you the next size up?" the saleswoman asks with a hopeful expression, like she thinks we might be getting out of her hair soon.

Natalie seems to consider this as she looks at herself in the mirror again. I can tell that she's not totally sold on this particular wedding gown, that it's not really her dream dress. But this isn't exactly a dream wedding either. And it's quite possible that the marriage will turn into a real nightmare. But selfishly I want to end the shopping now. I do not want to go looking for wedding dresses again.

"It looks so great on you," I tell Nat. "It's the best one you've tried on all day. Imagine it with your hair up...you'll look so elegant, so grown up."

Her eyes light up at this. "Grown up?"

I nod eagerly. "Yes, don't you think so, Caitlin?"

"It does make you look older..."

Nat holds her hair up with one hand and gives the dress one more long look. "Okay, I'll go ahead and try the next size up."

The saleswoman smiles. "I'll get it for you."

As it turns out, the larger size isn't that much bigger, but enough that we all think it'll be the best choice.

"And the price is really reasonable," I point out. "Even less than what your mom budgeted." I'm wearing the mossy green dress now. And I actually kind of like it.

Natalie turns around again, checking out her dress from every possible angle. Finally she tells me to come and stand beside her in front of the mirror. "I want to see how our dresses look together."

And so I do. But when I see the two of us standing side by side, it's hard not to laugh—or cry. With me in my flip-flops and Nat in the heels she brought from home, she towers nearly a foot above me.

"Hey, you went from the Great Pumpkin to the Little Green Sprout," she teases. So I stand on tiptoe now, which really doesn't help much. But at least I restrain myself from calling her the Jolly Cream Giant.

Caitlin laughs. "Kim can wear six-inch heels."

"Or maybe stilts," I add.

"It's not like you two will be standing right next to each other," Caitlin reminds us. "And at least Ben is tall, Nat. You two will look very regal together."

"Or you can just find yourself a taller maid of honor." Okay, I guess I'm feeling slightly miffed now. It's not like I can help being short. Or "vertically challenged" as my dad sometimes teases.

Nat turns and looks at me with a serious expression. "Why would I want anyone but you in my wedding, Little Sprout?"

I roll my eyes at her. But I suppose I do feel sort of touched. And it does occur to me that despite all these recent circumstances, Nat and I do go back a long way. We've been through a lot together, and it makes sense that I would be her maid of honor. Really, I guess I should be honored.

"Besides, Cesar's not that tall," she says. "You guys will be just right together."

"Is that who Ben finally decided on?" I ask.

"Yeah," she says. "Since Josh finally agreed to perform the ceremony. Ben and Cesar have really been getting close lately."

"This will be Josh's first wedding." Caitlin smiles in a way that suggests she's feeling proud of her husband. "Although Pastor Tony really had to twist his arm to get him to do it."

I suppress the urge to point out that it makes perfect sense for the youth pastor to perform the wedding ceremony for two seventeen-year-old youths. How appropriate.

Finally it's decided that Nat will get the creamy satin after all. And I will get the mossy green. She'll be the tall white lily, and I'll be the Little Green Sprout. "Although," I think to myself, "she's the one with the bulging pea in the pod."

As we're leaving the store and Natalie is gushing to Caitlin about how perfect everything is going to be and how much she appreciates her help and how great it will be to have Caitlin as her sister-in-law, I notice what I think is a shadow of doubt cross Caitlin's countenance. I'm guessing that, despite her sweet nature and positive attitude, she's still struggling with this marriage. Probably just as much as I am. After all, Ben is her little brother.

And although he has as much to do with Nat's pregnancy as Nat does, Caitlin must be feeling somewhat protective of him.

And as I sit in the backseat listening to them, I can't understand why one of the "adults" in either Ben or Natalie's lives hasn't put the brakes on this whole crazy thing. I mean, what are these people thinking? Even my dad is appalled by the craziness of it all. And it's not like it's his daughter getting married either. I seriously doubt he'd ever allow me to do something like this. Even if I were pregnant.

"Have you guys found a place to live yet?" I ask absently. Okay, maybe I do want to stir the pot just a little. Make Nat think a little further than just the big wedding day.

And I absolutely refuse to discuss the honeymoon with her, although she's already informed me that they'll probably stay in the mountains at a cabin that's owned by friends of Ben's family. She thinks it'll be so romantic.

But I'm imagining this rustic, animal-infested shack with a smelly outhouse and no running water. Okay, I'm a terrible excuse for a friend. But it's only because I love Nat, because I care about her future. And possibly because I'm a realist.

"Oh yeah, I meant to tell you. Josh's mom knows an older couple who needs house sitters until next spring," Caitlin says as she turns down the street where Nat and I live.

"Really?" Nat sounds hopeful.

"I think Josh gave Ben the number, and he's going to talk to them."

"That sounds good." Then Nat gets quiet. "But that would mean we couldn't really get settled...couldn't have our own things."

Okay, I'm wondering, what things? But I don't say this. I mean, I know that Nat and Ben have registered at a couple of stores. But from what I've heard from Nat's mom, the wedding's going to be pretty small. Which reminds me, I wonder if being maid of honor means I'm supposed to plan a wedding shower or something to that effect. I lean back into the seat and let out a little groan. When will the madness end?

"You okay?" asks Nat.

"Just a little carsick," I say, which isn't entirely untrue. I'm in a car and I feel sick.

"Almost there," says Caitlin.

Caitlin drops us off, and we both thank her. I make a mental note to call her later for some wedding shower advice. Sheesh, I'm only seventeen. I shouldn't have to be doing all of this. Of course, as I walk into the house, I realize that Nat shouldn't either. But it seems like she's actually enjoying it.

I halfheartedly show Dad my dress, and although he says it's pretty and that I'll be a beautiful maid of honor, I can tell he's not pleased.

"I know, I know," I say as I lay the dress over the back of our new leather couch in the family room. Dad and I replaced a few things—in an effort to move on in our grieving process over Mom. "Everything about this wedding feels all wrong to me too."

"It seems like a hard way to start a life together...getting married because of a baby. I just don't know..."

And suddenly I remember my grandma, Dad's mom, and the surprising story she told me down in Florida last summer. I look at Dad and wonder if it's the right time to tell him about this. But he's replaced his reading glasses and is already opening his book again. Maybe some other time.

I carry my dress up to my room and hang it in the back of my closet so I don't have to look at it every day and be reminded of how my best friend is ruining her life.

Then I do a double check on the things I've already laid out for school. Okay, it's true, I've even picked out the outfit I plan to wear tomorrow. Although I reserve the right to change my mind if the weather cools down. Anyway, everything seems to be in good order. So I decide to check my e-mail and maybe answer a letter for my column. Since the e-mail is disappointing, I go with the latter, reading through about a dozen letters before I settle on this.

Dear Jamie,

My mom has been married six times, so far. My dad was number two in the lineup, and they got divorced when I was a baby. Her marriages last two to three years, although they seem to be getting shorter. And every time she gets engaged, she says, "This one is going to be the one." Anyway, she's about to get married again. She calls this dude her "lucky number seven," but I can tell he's a loser like the rest. I'm seventeen and this will be my senior year, but I'm sick of this game. I'd like to move out, but I'm not sure I can handle it. I have a part-time job, but I don't know if it's enough to support myself with. What should I do?

Tired of Stepdads

Dear Tired,

I can understand your frustration. But I can also understand your hesitancy to move out. Here are my questions for you: 1) Is there another relative who you might live with during your last year of high school? 2) Or do you have a good friend with understanding parents who might let you stay with them? 3) If you really want to move out, do you have enough money for a rental deposit? 4) Have you estimated what it will cost each month, making a budget that includes things like rent, food, utilities, clothing, commuting costs, etc.? 5) Have you asked a school or church counselor for advice? 6) Last but not least, have you told your mother how you feel—have you asked for her help in making this adjustment?

I know that being on your own looks tempting right now, but it could end up being like jumping from the frying pan into the fire. Maybe you should do what you can to get yourself ready to move out (like saving and planning a budget) while you give yourself time to see whether or not your mom has made another mistake.

Just Jamie

Two

Friday, September 8

I just finished the first week of my senior year, and as far as academics go, I think it's going to be easy breezy. I've already taken most of my requirements as well as several AP classes, and I could actually graduate early if I want. Not that I want to.

The only reason I'm even thinking about this is because that's what Natalie plans to do. She met with the academic counselor this week. And her new plan is to finish high school before the baby comes. Fortunately, like me, she's taken almost all of her requirements, and by taking a full load of classes this term, as well as one night class at the community college, she can be done by Christmas.

"Of course, I'll come back and walk with my class for graduation," she informed me at lunch the other day. "But I think it's better to do it like this."

And while the selfish side of me wants to argue this point with her, I know she's right. Unfortunately, the first week of her senior year has been anything but easy breezy. And despite the negative feelings I've harbored toward my best friend lately, I'm feeling really sorry about that and actually pretty defensive of her now.

Naturally the word's leaking out. Okay, it's more like a dam that has burst wide open. By the end of this week, the only people who don't know about the pregnancy and upcoming marriage of Nat and Ben must be living under a stone. But the comments I've overheard and the looks I've observed—toward Nat, not Ben—have been nothing short of downright mean and cruel.

The weird and sad thing is how quickly our classmates put their own spin on this regrettable story. Acting like Nat got pregnant on purpose, like it's her way to catch poor Benjamin O'Conner. Like Ben is some innocent, unsuspecting victim who got pulled into Natalie's diabolical scheme. Give me a break!

It doesn't help matters that Ben seems to be avoiding Nat. He told her he's just trying to lay low until the news dies down. Poor Ben. I really do feel sorry for him too. Life as he knew it is pretty much over now. He doesn't get to play sports this year, and although he acts like it's no big deal, I know it's got to hurt. He's been such a jock in the past. Nat said he's thinking about graduating early too, although he doesn't have quite the academic record Nat has and will need to take more community college classes.

To make matters worse, some kids are throwing Natalie's religion in her face, making fun of her for messing up, even calling her a hypocrite. Some do it behind her back. Some to her face.

"I hate this school!" Nat slams the door of my Jeep. It's Friday afternoon, and as usual, I'm giving her a ride home.

"Give them time," I say. I want to tell her not to take it out on poor Daisy (my Jeep), but considering her mood I think better of this. "In a week or so, they'll have something new to gossip about."

"I can't wait to get out of here," she says as I pull out of the school parking lot. "For good."

I don't tell her that I'm feeling slightly abandoned by this announcement. Or remind her that when she leaves school, she's leaving me too. Of course, I could easily graduate early myself. But I was actually hoping to finish this year in style. And it's no secret that I have a chance at being valedictorian. Not that it's such a big thing. But I do remember how Mom always thought I would get it. And I guess I'd like to do it for her. Graduating early would wipe out those chances.

"How's Ben doing?" I ask, hoping to change the subject to something she likes better. But she just shrugs.

"Everything okay with you two?"

Again with the shrug. "We haven't talked much lately."

"I don't mean to be intrusive," I say, "but if you're getting married in, what, like two weeks? Well, shouldn't you two be talking?"

And then Nat bursts into tears.

Oh, great. I try not to be too distracted as I navigate my way through traffic. I mean, getting in a wreck won't help matters. Finally I decide to stop at the mini mart and get us both a cold drink. I ask her what she wants and then go inside to get it, relieved to be away from her for a few minutes.

As I wait at the cash register, I try to figure out something to say to her. I mean, Nat knows that underneath my maid-of-honor good attitude (well, for the most part) I seriously question this marriage. But I also know that it's not my life, not my decision. And I can't exactly go out there and tell her she's making a huge mistake. Still, I can't help but think I should be willing to say something.

"Here's your change," the woman tells me.

I thank her and pick up the drinks, and as I walk back outside I silently pray. I ask God to give me words for Nat—whether they're words of encouragement or warning, that they will be wrapped in love. I want to be willing to be used however God would use me.

"Here you go," I say cheerfully as I hand her a drink.

"Thanks." Nat gives me a wet-looking smile. "Sorry about that. I mean, losing it with you. I guess emotions can get a little whacked out when you're pregnant."

"No, it's okay," I say as I get in. "And you must be

under a lot of stress too. There's a lot going on in your life."

She nods and takes a sip. "You got that right. And hearing all the snide remarks at school this week, well, it doesn't make things any easier."

"Yeah, I know." Okay, I'm trying to be understanding, trying to hear what God would have me say to my friend.

"And then there's my mom..."

"What's up there?"

"It's like she's going to be mad at me forever." Nat sniffs. "I mean, she's supposed to be a Christian, but honestly, I don't feel much forgiveness from that woman."

"Oh..."

And Nat goes on and on, finally settling on Ben. "He missed our premarriage counseling appointment with Pastor Tony last night." She starts to cry again. "And he hasn't talked to me all day." She turns and looks at me. "Do you think he's changed his mind?"

Okay, I'm sorry, but I start to feel a tiny bit hopeful just now. Although I try not to show it. "I don't know..."

"What would I do, Kim?" Her eyes are wide with fear now. "If he backed out, I mean? <u>What would I do</u>?"

I consider my answer. "Well...you know that I happen to think adoption is a pretty good option for some children."

I can tell she's about to get mad at me, to overreact, but then it's like she's trying to control herself too. She just slowly nods. "Yeah, it's worked out okay for you."

"Okay?" I echo. "I think it's been great. I mean, consider the alternatives. I could've remained in an impoverished Korean orphanage. Or worse yet, what if my mother had kept me and what if she was a hooker and what if I'd been forced to grow up in some horrible—"

"I'm not a hooker, Kim."

"That's not what I mean. But seriously, Nat, how hard would it be to be a teen mom, barely finished with high school and trying to raise a baby and support yourself totally on your own?"

She looks down at her drink. "I know..."

Although I know it could get me in trouble, I decide to take the next step. "And it wasn't that long ago that you wanted to get rid of the baby completely. Remember? But wouldn't it be much braver of you, and much better for the baby, to allow some really good parents, people who have a good home and money and everything, to raise this child?"

I can tell she's thinking about this, but she doesn't say anything.

"I know that I'm really thankful my birth mother did that much for me. And my parents were thankful too."

Now she sits up straighter, and I can see this look in her eyes, this look that's slightly hard and cold and somewhat calculated. "Ben promised to marry me. He said he wants to be a father to our baby. He knows it's the right thing to do." She pushes her hair out of her face. "And that's what's going to happen. Even if it looks bad and dark right now, I know God is going to work this out for good. I just need to have faith, Kim. And that's what I plan to do."

Well, that seems to end our conversation, which is a good thing since it's getting pretty hot in the Jeep now. So I start up the engine and drive us home in a silence so thick I can feel it pressing against me.

"Thanks for the ride," she says in a stiff voice as I stop in front of her house.

"No problem." Then I drive a couple houses down to my house, get out of my Jeep, and now I slam the door. Poor Daisy.

There's a message from Caitlin on our answering machine. She's helping me plan Nat's bridal shower, which is supposed to be at my house, but at the moment I'm not feeling too enthusiastic about it. Even so, I call Caitlin back. And I guess she senses that all's not well by the edgy tone of my voice.

"I'm sorry, but I just dropped Nat at home and she's making me crazy."

"What's up?"

Since Caitlin and I have already discussed this, and since she's Ben's sister and has promised me confidentiality, I feel fairly safe telling her. Without going into all the gory details, I admit that I still think this marriage is a great big mistake. I also tell her how I probably offended Nat by bringing up the adoption option again. "I really blew it."

"You shouldn't feel sorry about that," Caitlin says. "And Nat should respect your advice."

"I'm worried about her," I finally say. "The scariest part of this whole thing is the way she believes that if they get married—or as she says, 'do the right thing'—they'll automatically be blessed and live happily ever after. Like God is going to miraculously make everything wonderful. But I think it's going to be hard. Really hard. Their chances of making a marriage work are pretty slim. And if it doesn't work...well, where does that leave Nat? She'll be stuck with a baby and nothing more than a high school diploma. Where do you go from there?"

"I know..."

"You do?"

"I've got an idea, Kim."

"What?"

"Oh, it might be crazy. But it just might be a good wake-up call for Nat too."

Then she tells me about one of her high school friends and how this girl got married when she was just a little older than Nat and under some very similar circumstances.

"That first year was really hard on Anna and Joel," she continues. "And they've struggled ever since. They just had their second baby in June, and shortly after that, well, Joel decided to call it quits. He left Anna a couple months ago. According to Anna, it's hopeless. She sounds fairly certain that they'll be divorced before Christmas."

"That's too bad."

"I know. It's really sad. And Anna's so sweet and so smart. But she's so stuck too. She never finished college either. She worked to support them while Joel finished up and finally graduated. Anna's working at a restaurant now."

"So what's your idea?"

"Anna just moved back to town last month, and I thought maybe we could take Nat to visit her. Let Nat see for herself how something like this can turn out."

"Do you really think it'll work?" Okay, I'm thinking this sounds like a good plan, but how will we get Nat to go along with it? Won't she know that it's a setup from the get-go?

"This is how we'll present it. I'll tell Natalie that Anna's a young mom too, that she's just moved back to town and doesn't really know any other young moms around here, and that I want to introduce them. I'll also ask Nat to encourage Anna to come back to church. She used to go to Faith Fellowship, but now she doesn't go anywhere. She says she's too busy."

"That'll be perfect," I say. "Give Nat a mission to get Anna to church, and she'll be all over it."

"Okay. Maybe we can even pull this off tomorrow. I'll give Anna a call tonight and see how her schedule looks."

"Great. Let me know."

"And how about I just e-mail you the list of names and phone numbers of the ladies for the shower," Caitlin says finally. "You'll want to call them ASAP if we're going to do the shower by next weekend."

"Maybe things will change by then. Maybe we won't need a bridal shower after all."

"Better be prepared just in case," she warns me.

Even so, I decide that I also better keep the receipts for anything I get for the shower (other than perishable items, and I'll wait until the last minute to get those anyway) so that if Natalie should come to her senses, I'll be ready to return everything. A girl can hope. I've already saved the receipt from my dress, and as much as I hate returning anything, I'd happily become the Queen of Returns if it meant Natalie avoided making what I think will be the biggest mistake of her life. Okay, maybe the second biggest mistake.

Dear Jamie,

My best friend doesn't want to be friends anymore. When I call her, she hangs up. When I try to talk to her at school, she just snubs me. I don't know what's wrong, but it's really hurting my feelings. On top of this, she's started gossiping about me behind my back. I'm so mad at her that I'm thinking about getting even. I could tell everyone some things about her. Like how she used to wet the bed. I know that sounds mean, but that's how she's treating me. What should I do?

Fighting Mad

Dear FM,

You need to get to the bottom of this and find out why your friend is angry at you. If you honestly can't think of anything you did to hurt her, you need to come up with a way to talk to her. Why don't you write her a note, telling her how badly you feel and asking her what it is that went wrong and if she could make time to talk to you? And if that doesn't work, I suggest you just move on. Find a new friend. And, for sure, do NOT tell anyone about your friend's old secrets. Besides hurting her, it will make you look like a bad friend.

Just Jamie

Three

Sunday, September 10

Caitlin, Nat, and I went to visit Anna after church today. And it was pretty strange. At one point, I wished I'd bowed out of this weird little scheme altogether. But on the other hand, I guess I was glad to see what Anna's life is really like. Not that I'm planning on getting married and having kids anytime soon, but just as a point of reference.

Anna was really nice. And I could tell she was hurting. But it was sweet of her to let us into her world. I suspect that Caitlin had explained the circumstances beforehand. Even so, I'm not sure I could've been as transparent as Anna was. If I were in her shoes, I mean.

She and her mom (who, according to Caitlin, is actually her grandmother) share this tiny apartment that's not in a very nice part of town. And although Anna knew we were coming, it didn't look like much effort had gone into straightening things up. But then her kids are pretty small and into everything, and I suppose she was tired from work. Or maybe she just wanted to shock Natalie. Not a bad idea, really.

"Come in," she tells us as she opens the door. She's holding a baby who's crying, and a toddler is clinging to her leg. "This is Hannah." She nods down at the little girl with the same mocha-colored skin as her mother. She leads us through the cramped and cluttered space. "And this is Ruthie." She holds the fussing baby out for us to see.

"Oh! She is so sweet. May I hold her?"

Anna smiles at Caitlin and hands the baby over. "Most definitely."

Then Caitlin introduces us to Anna. "Like I said on the phone, Natalie's going to be my new sister-in-law, and her baby is due in January. Kim is her best friend."

"Sit down." Anna removes a laundry basket and some toys from the couch. "I would've cleaned up, but I worked the late shift last night, and then Ruthie was fussy all night, and well..."

"Don't apologize," Caitlin says.

"Yeah," I agree. "It looks like you have your hands full."

She nods. "My mom and I both work. We alternate our shifts so we can take turns watching the girls."

"That must be hard." Caitlin gently jiggles Ruthie, soothing her fussiness as if she really knows how to do this. And then I remember that she has worked at an orphanage in Mexico. I guess that gave her some experience.

"Not as hard as when I had to do it on my own," Anna admits. Hannah has crawled into her mom's lap now, snuggling up as if to show us that she belongs there. It's really kind of sweet. "When Joel was in school and I was working, I had to do pretty much everything myself."

"Joel didn't help?" Caitlin asks.

Anna just laughs, but there's a bitter edge to it. "Unfortunately for me, Joel's one of those old-school guys—thinking the little woman should take care of the kids, the house, all that sort of thing."

Caitlin shakes her head. "Too bad."

Now I notice how Nat's not saying anything. In fact, she looks a bit like that proverbial deer in the headlights. Does she see her life flashing before her eyes?

"What are your plans?" Caitlin asks. "I mean, like going back to school?"

Anna laughs again, but again there's a cynical sound to it, and it seems to fight against her sweet-looking face and her kind eyes. "Yeah, right."

"You could probably get an academic scholarship," Caitlin says. "You were always so smart, Anna. You had a scholarship before."

"Before..." she sighs. "Before Hannah and Ruthie came along."

"But even the community college," Caitlin continues,

"has a childcare program and everything."

"Do you know how long that waiting list is?" Anna rolls her dark eyes.

"But you could at least get on it."

Anna seems to consider this. "Yeah...I guess I could."

"It'd be worth it, Anna," Caitlin says with emphasis. "In the long run."

Anna nods. "I know you're right, Caitlin. It's just so hard to see beyond the daily grind right now. I mean, if you knew what my schedule was like..." Then she proceeds to tell us how she goes to work, comes home exhausted, tries to catch up on laundry and household chores, sleeps...and then nurses the baby, changes diapers, cleans up messes, deals with Hannah.

"I thought the terrible twos were bad," she tells us. "Now we're in the fearsome fours." But she smiles as she says this, taking a moment to stroke Hannah's curly hair. "Not that I'd trade her for anything." Hannah looks up. "You're Mommy's helper, aren't you?"

Hannah nods and smiles.

"How old is your baby?" asks Nat, the first words she's spoken since we got there.

"Almost three months." Anna sighs. "Hopefully she'll be out of the colicky stage soon."

"What's that?" asks Nat.

"Colic?" Anna looks at Nat with raised brows, then kind of laughs. "I guess that's a good question since most experts don't exactly agree on its cause or its treatment. Let's just say it has something to do with digestion, and most babies have it at least for a while. You'll find out about it for yourself soon enough."

Nat looks terrified as Anna continues.

"The main problem with colic is that it involves a lot of crying that's hard to stop. It can get really frustrating. Although Hannah had it worse than Ruthie. But then I found this great book with some ideas that actually seem to work. The doctor calls them the five S's."

"What's that?" Nat asks.

"Swaddling, swinging, shushing, sucking..." Anna frowns. "I keep forgetting the fifth one."

Nat looks thoroughly confused now. Almost as if Anna is speaking a foreign language. Maybe she is—motherese.

"Don't worry," Anna assures her. "It'll start to make sense once the little one arrives. Do you know what you're having?"

Nat blinks, then seems to recover. "Oh, you mean whether it's a boy or girl? No, we decided we want to wait to find out."

"And how is Ben doing with all this?" Anna asks.

"He wants to do the right thing," Natalie says in a crisp voice. "He wants to be a good father to his baby."

Anna looks skeptical.

"It's not easy for him," Caitlin adds. "But he's really trying to do what he believes God is calling him to do. He wants to be responsible."

The conversation switches from Ben back to babies. Anna tries to get Nat to talk about ways she's getting ready to be a mother, but Nat is being pretty resistant, almost as if she doesn't really believe that she will eventually have a baby in her arms. Sad as this sounds, it gives me hope.

Then the baby starts to really fuss, and Anna announces that it's feeding time. Taking the baby from Caitlin, she pulls up her T-shirt and starts breast-feeding Ruthie right in front of us. Now, okay, I know this a natural thing and probably very good for babies, but I'm thinking "Eew!" and I have to look away. I am relieved to see that Nat is uncomfortable too. Caitlin is the only one who continues chatting with Anna as if this is no big deal. And maybe it's not. But it's not exactly in my comfort zone either.

Finally Ruthie's done with both sides, and now Hannah is starting to act up. "I think it's nap time," Anna tells us.

"We'll get out of your hair," Caitlin says, standing. "But hopefully you and Nat can stay in touch, and if Nat has questions, maybe she can come to you?"

"And I can loan you that book," Anna tells Nat. "And if you have a girl, I can give you lots of clothes. Joel's mom is a shopping freak. She keeps the girls looking good in little OshKoshes and all sorts of things."

"Yeah," says Nat. "That'd be great."

"And maybe we'll see you at church?" Caitlin asks hopefully.

"Maybe when life settles down a little." Anna nods. "I know it would be good to get back into it. And I know the girls would be better off growing up in a church." She looks at Caitlin with tears in her eyes. "I just thought it was going to be different than this."

Caitlin reaches out and hugs her old friend. "You're going to be fine, Anna. But this is a time when you need the strength of a church behind you. And like I said, Josh and I really want to have you and the girls over for a meal, when you're ready."

Anna nods again. "Yeah, I know. It's just that the adjustment and everything...well, it's just been a lot harder than I expected."

"You have friends, Anna," Caitlin tells her. "Friends who are ready to help."

Anna smiles now. "Thanks."

After we go, Natalie is pretty quiet. I'm sure this has given her plenty to think about.

"I like Anna," I say as Caitlin drives us back to where I left my Jeep at the church parking lot. "She seems really nice."

"She is," Caitlin agrees. "But she's not really up to her usual spunky self. I'm sure it's pretty tiring doing all that she has to do."

"I can't even imagine," I say. "When she talked about getting woken up in the middle of the night? Man, I would not be good at that."

Caitlin laughs. "I guess it's something moms just have to get used to."

"I know what you guys are doing," Natalie says suddenly.

"What?" Caitlin glances over at her.

"Trying to scare me."

"No..." Caitlin says in a kind voice. "But it's true that I wanted you to see what it's like being a young mom. And that it can be hard."

"But I won't be single like Anna," Nat tosses back.

"I hope not," Caitlin tells her. "But there are no guaranties. Anna didn't think she'd be single either. It came as a shock to everyone. I mean, it's like they'd gotten through the hardest part—Joel had graduated from college. Life should've been getting better. And then he just left."

"I wonder why," I say.

"Josh thinks it's because they got married so young, had kids too soon. He's talked to Joel about it a couple of times, and although Joel feels bad and says that he'll pay child support, he also is tired of being a husband and a dad."

"He probably has a girlfriend," Natalie throws in.

"That's what I thought too," Caitlin says. "But Anna said he doesn't. And when Josh asked Joel, he denied it too."

"Well, maybe they'll get back together," says Nat.

"That's what we're hoping. Josh is trying to talk Joel into getting counseling."

By the time we're back at the church, I'm not sure if Caitlin has gotten through to Nat or not. And when Nat and I are in my Jeep, I think the whole thing might've been for nothing.

"It's going to be different with Ben and me," she says as she buckles the seat belt over her thicker-than-usual waist.

"What makes you so sure?" I ask.

"It's just a God-thing," she says.

I don't remind her that Anna and Joel are Christians too. That they thought things were going to go better for them. What's the use, I wonder as I drive us home. In the end, Nat will do what Nat wants and say that it's God's will. Okay, I know that's kind of harsh and judgmental on my part, but I'm beginning to think that's how it is. Even so, I will continue praying for my friend. And I will continue getting ready for her bridal shower.

Saturday, September 16

If I never give another bridal shower in my entire life, it will be way too soon. And if Nat thinks I'm going to give her a baby shower, well, she can think again!

Thank goodness for Caitlin today. I would've been lost without her. She managed to keep things light and happy, acting like it was perfectly normal for two seventeen-year-olds to get married and set up house. Speaking of setting up house, it turns out that Ben and Nat will not be house-sitting for Josh's parents' friends. When the older couple heard there was a baby involved, they backed out.

"Did you see all the cool stuff I got?" Natalie asks as I help her carry things over to her house.

"Yeah," I say in a flat-sounding voice.

"You were back in the kitchen so much, I wasn't sure."

"There was a lot to do," I say. "And Caitlin was doing a great job of keeping things going with the ladies."

"Caitlin is such a natural hostess," Nat says as she opens the door to her house. "I'm so lucky that she's going to be my sister-in-law." She laughs. "I guess I should say 'blessed' since luck really has nothing to do with it."

Unless you mean bad luck, I'm thinking.

"Is that the last of it?" Mrs. McCabe asks as we haul the stuff into the dining room.

"I think so," I tell her. "If I see anything we missed, I'll bring it over."

"Thank you for doing this for Natalie," Mrs. McCabe tells me in a rather automated sounding voice. It's pretty much the tone she's been using about anything to do with Nat or the wedding or the baby. It's like she's holding everything in, and I don't think I'd like to be around when she finally lets it all out.

"No problem," I tell her.

"Yes, thanks!" Nat throws her arms around me in a hug. "You're the best friend ever."

I'm tempted to point out that I'm really rotten underneath and that I have very little hope for the upcoming marriage of Nat and Ben, but what would be the point? "Well, I'd better get back and clean things up before my dad comes home."

Nat lets out a big yawn. "And I think I'll take a nap. All this excitement has worn me out."

Mrs. McCabe just frowns. And I make a hasty exit.

The house is quiet when I get home. And for a change, it feels welcome. All the voices and the women and the presents...well, it just felt so wrong. And I'm glad it's over. I get a garbage bag and go around gathering up paper plates and cups and napkins—all in the fall colors Natalie requested, but looking more like wilted leaves now. I put the furniture back into their regular places, give the kitchen a quick wipe down, and am just heading to my room when my dad gets home.

"Safe to come in?" he asks.

"The women have all gone home."

He smiles and gives me a hug. "How did it go?"

I offer him a piece of leftover cake and then proceed to tell him how it really went. No smoothing, glossing, pretending. And by the time I finish, he's laughing.

"Poor Kimmy."

I nod, appreciating his pity. "And next week is the wedding!"

"Good cake," he says as he hands me his empty plate.

"Do you think I'll ever have a normal life again?"

He considers this. "Is there really such a thing?"

"Things used to feel normal," I remind him. "When

Mom was here, back before Natalie got pregnant. Life was pretty calm and peaceful."

"Yes. Maybe we took it for granted."

I sigh. "Like you don't know what you've got until it's gone..."

He nods. "I hate to break up our little party, but unless you need anything, I've got some work to finish up."

"You and me both," I say. But as I go to my room, I'm still thinking about what he said. Maybe we did take "normal" for granted. Maybe we all do.

Dear Jamie,

About ten years ago, I did something really horrible. And it never seems to leave me alone. I've never told anyone, and I'm not even sure if I can tell you. But I'll try. When I was about five years old and my little brother was two, I was supposed to be watching him for my mom. It was summer and we were playing outside. But he kept bugging me while I was digging in the sandbox, and I told him to go away and leave me alone. I don't know how long he was gone, but when I went to look for him, I found him in our wading pool, face down. And I just stood there for a long time. I thought he was holding his breath, playing a trick on me. I can't even remember what happened next. But my brother drowned that day. My parents said it wasn't my fault, but I know how I told him to go away, and then I never even pulled him out of the pool. Sometimes I feel like I'm going to explode, like I can't keep this in anymore. What should I do?

Murderer

Wow, this is a heartbreaker. I ask God to help me with it.

Dear M,

First of all, you are NOT a murderer. Second of all, your parents were ABSOLUTELY RIGHT—it was not your fault. No five-year-old should be responsible for watching a two-year-old, and I'm guessing your mom feels way worse than you do about the loss of your brother. Guilt can do horrible things to people, and I'm guessing this tragedy has hurt your family more than you even know. I suggest that you all get counseling, together and individually. You need to get over this and move on with your life, and it will probably take professional help to do this. I also suggest that you talk to God about how you're feeling. His forgiveness goes much deeper than the human kind—and, in time, I believe God is the one who can heal your aching heart.

Just Jamie

Four

Friday, September 22

As usual, I gave Nat a ride home today. I suppose Ben would do this, but he got a full-time job last week. He cut back on his class load. Not so much that it will jeopardize his diploma, but just enough that he can work the swing shift at his dad's office building—forty hours a week. Not in advertising like Mr. O'Conner, but as a maintenance man who scrubs toilets and mops floors.

Nat says he has to wear these gray striped coveralls and weird shoes, but she thinks he looks cute in this new uniform. Just the same, I'm guessing it's a little humiliating for someone like Ben O'Conner. Not exactly like wearing your football jersey on game days, like today. Maybe Ben was relieved not to be at school all day. It must be hard seeing his jock friends doing their regular thing while he's stepping into a whole different life.

"Ben doesn't have to work tonight," Nat tells me when I pull in front of her house.

"Big bachelor party?" I ask in a somewhat sarcastic tone.

"No, but Cesar is getting some of the guys from church together," she says with slight exasperation, which I'm sure is meant for me. "No strippers or girls popping out of cakes."

"That's good to know."

"But what about me?" she says.

"What about you?" I toss back.

"Well, you're my maid of honor...seems like you should do something special for me."

I let out an involuntary groan.

"Kim Peterson!" She's frowning now. "You don't have to be such a wet blanket."

"Well..." I begin, "I did just give you a bridal shower last week."

She softens a little. "I know and that was nice. But this is my last night being a single girl, and besides we don't even have a rehearsal or a rehearsal dinner or anything tonight."

I control myself from rolling my eyes or saying something really regrettable. Like, what does she expect? It's not like you can blame her mom for putting some stops on this comedy of errors. Nat already admitted that, even without the frills, it's costing too much.

"So?" I ask, knowing how stubborn Nat can be. "I'm not exactly experienced at this kind of thing. What would you suggest?"

"I don't know..."

"Pizza and videos?"

She kind of shrugs.

"Look, Nat..." I hear the edge in my voice now. "This isn't exactly your normal kind of wedding situation, you know? Do you want me to call a bunch of girls from high school and invite them to come over and party?"

She sadly shakes her head. "Pizza and videos will be fine."

Now I feel guilty. "I'll get some ice cream too. And you can spend the night if you want."

She brightens now. "Okay, this is sounding better and better."

"Around sixish?"

"I'll be there. Maybe we can do pedicures and facials and stuff. Get all prettied up for the wedding."

I force what I hope looks like a genuine smile. "Sounds great!"

I do my part, foraging through the video store for Nat's favorite old movies and then over to Safeway in search of her favorite cookies 'n' cream ice cream, finally swinging by Pizza Hut to pick up our order. By the time I get home, Nat is already there. And I can tell by my dad's expression that he's relieved to see me.

"There she is now," he says in an overly jovial voice. "I told you she wouldn't be long. You know how punctual our Kimmy is." He winks at me. "Now if you ladies will excuse me."

"You mean you don't want to stick around for a pedicure?" I tease as I set the pizza box on the counter.

"No, but I might sneak a piece of this..." He peeks in the box.

"There's plenty," I say as I put the ice cream in the freezer. "It's a giant."

"Ooh, you got my favorite." Nat snags a piece.

"Nothing but the best for the bride-to-be," I say, trying to keep my voice light. I've been reminding myself of how cheerful Caitlin was at the shower last week. And really, what can it hurt to put on a happy face?

Now it's midnight, and after pizza, ice cream, movies, facials, pedicures, manicures, even some eyebrow plucking, Natalie, "the bride-to-be," has finally dozed off, and I'm sitting here in front of my computer trying to make some sense of my life. But it seems I can't.

Okay, there's one thing I learned tonight. I think Caitlin is on to something. Here's the deal. I had what I thought could be an excruciatingly painful evening to get through, and I could've done it in my usual complaining sort of way. But following Caitlin's example, I decided to take the "high road." I did an attitude adjustment, put on a smile, and guess what? It wasn't so bad. In fact, it was actually sort of fun.

And—I reminded myself—after tonight, Nat will be a married woman, and we won't really be having times like this anymore. Okay, as weird as that sounded at first, after it sunk in, it really made me kind of sad. Now, as Nat is snoozing, I'm thinking about how I'm going to miss my best friend. Even though she's been a royal pain lately, I really do love her. I really want the best for her life. And so, after we were sort of done for the evening, I told her that I wanted us to pray together.

"Pray together?" She blinked in surprise. "You and me?"

"Yeah...I want us to pray for you and Ben. For the wedding tomorrow and for your future and for the future of your unborn child. Is that okay?"

"Of course."

And so we prayed. And it was really sweet. When I finished, Nat told me that it was the best bachelorette party ever. Of course, I wondered what she could really compare it to, but I didn't mention this. Still, as I sit here writing in my diary, I have to wonder how it's going to go with Nat and Ben. Oh, I don't mean the wedding. Knowing Caitlin, it will probably go smoothly enough. I mean what comes after the wedding. What then?

Nat said that Ben found them a little place to live. It's downtown, close to his work, but she'll have to ride a bus to school. His parents helped him with the rent deposit as well as some of the other starting expenses. But that ends now. "But with his job," she assured me, "we'll probably be okay."

I didn't ask her about things like health insurance or baby expenses. I mean, what do I know about things like that? Still, my practical side wonders. But it's the night before her wedding...why should I be the one to rain on her parade? Especially when I already know that tomorrow's forecast is for "scattered showers"?

Sunday, September 24

Well, at least it didn't rain yesterday. And all things considered, I guess the wedding went fairly well. It was a little unnerving when Natalie's wedding gown was too tight to zip, but with some help from Caitlin and Steph, we finally managed to fit her into it.

"But you'd better get right out of it after the reception," Steph warns Nat.

"Will it hurt the baby?" Caitlin asked with concern.

Steph laughed. "No, but she might split a seam."

Caitlin's grandmother-in-law did a nice job on the flowers. Even nicer than a florist, I was thinking as Cesar and I got in place to take our walk down the aisle. The music was playing, and I could see Ben standing up there by Josh. And although Josh was smiling and looking fairly comfortable with what was his first wedding, Ben looked like a lamb on his way to the slaughter. Seriously, he looked like he'd give anything to be anywhere but here. Even as Cesar escorted me down the aisle, I half expected Ben to make a mad dash for the nearest exit. But somehow he stayed in place. Maybe Josh had superglued his feet to the floor.

The crowd was small. Maybe forty, or even less. Just close family members and friends from church. I was glad that my dad came. He'd been saying he wasn't sure. And he'd even politely declined Natalie's invitation to walk her down the aisle. Fortunately she had an uncle who was willing.

Then the bridal march music began, and Natalie and her uncle started coming down the aisle. And to my surprise, I began to cry. Now I realize that lots of people cry at weddings. And I figure it's because they are moved or touched. But the reason I was crying was because it all seemed so hopeless. And seeing my beautiful best friend in her too-tight dress, in a church that was mostly empty, with such a small wedding party...well, it just seemed so pathetic. And wrong.

But I forced a smile as she got closer, and I'm sure she thought they were tears of joy as I held her bouquet and waited for Ben and her to exchange vows and rings. Their rings are very simple gold bands. Not cheap. But not fancy either.

"Someday he'll get me a diamond," Natalie told me when we were doing manicures the night before.

Well, for her sake, I hope that's true. But after the reception, when we told them good-bye in front of the church and I watched them driving away in Ben's little car... Well, I just felt sad.

"They'll be okay," my dad told me as he came up and put his arm around me.

I turned and studied him. "Really? Do you think so?"

"Or not." He smiled at me. "But things work out."

And so as we drove home from Natalie's wedding, I

told him about the story his mother had told me when I was in Florida. I told him about how she and my dad's father fell in love during World War II, how they planned to get married but didn't. And how hard it was when he died and she was pregnant. But how she pretended to be a widow, and no one ever really knew.

Dad nodded as he turned into our driveway. "I think I sort of knew that, Kim."

"Really? She said she never told you."

"I know. I guess I just suspected something."

"Does it bother you?"

He just shook his head. "I can understand why she'd do that. Times were different then. Unwed mothers weren't socially acceptable."

"Do you think times have changed that much?" I asked as we got out of the car.

"In some ways."

"Do you think it would've been better if Nat and Ben hadn't gotten married?"

He turned and looked at me. "What do you think, Kimmy?"

I didn't answer, but I felt sure that we both knew what the other thought—and that it was the same.

"Someday it's going to be your wedding, sweetheart," he said as we went into the house. "And we're going to have us one big barn burner of a wedding!"

"All right!"

The radio was still playing in the kitchen, probably

from this morning. But it was on one of the oldies stations my mom liked to tune into. Then my dad bowed. "May I have this dance?"

I held out my mossy green skirt in a curtsy. "Certainly."

And as my dad and I danced within the small confines of the kitchen, I promised myself that one day we would dance at my wedding. And, I promised myself, for the sake of my mom and my dad—and for myself—I would do it right. And that means doing it God's way.

Dear Jamie,

My older sister is sixteen and doesn't even have her driver's license yet, but she's been sneaking my mom's car out at night. She bribes me by giving me rides sometimes, but I'm starting to get scared that we'll get caught. I can't believe my mom hasn't figured this out yet, and I've almost told her a couple of times, but then my sister would probably kill me. What should I do?

Stuck

Dear Stuck,

You're in a hard place. But if you consider the consequences, it might be easier to do the right thing. For instance, if your sister got into a wreck, she would, at the very least, be in trouble with the law and probably lose her right to legally drive for a long time. And at the very worst, someone could get seriously hurt or even killed. There's a reason that people have to be tested to get a driver's license. But besides that, what about your mom? How would she feel knowing that her children are doing something like this behind her back? What do you think you should do? I think you already know the answer. And, sure, your sister might get mad at you, but she won't kill you.

Just Jamie

Five

Friday, September 29

As far as I know, and I'm not asking questions, Nat and Ben's honeymoon went just fine. They only got to spend two nights at the cabin, and both of them were back in school by Tuesday. Of course, since lots of the kids knew about "the big wedding," there's been plenty of teasing and crud going on. But I have to give it to Nat and Ben, they're taking it pretty well. Although Nat's patience was wearing thin by the end of the week.

"Some people need to get a life," she told me at lunch today.

"Give them time," I said. "They'll get bored with the O'Conners before long."

"Yeah, at least until I really start showing. That should get them going again." She sighed loudly. "Which brings me to something..."

"Huh?" I looked at her. Like what was she getting at?

"I'm thinking about switching schools."

"Switching?"

"Yeah. Mrs. Harper was the one who first suggested it. She told me about this place downtown. Actually, it's close to our apartment. Anyway, it's for pregnant teen girls. You can get your diploma and even bring your baby to school."

"But you could get your diploma here before the baby is born," I reminded her.

"I know..." She looked around the cafeteria. "But it's hard being here. I feel like such a misfit."

"We've always been misfits, Nat."

"But it's worse now." She looked right at me then. "And I know it's not easy for you."

Okay, this surprised me. I wasn't used to having Nat consider my feelings.

"I think it's for the best," she finally said.

"But I'm going to miss you."

"We'll still see each other, Kim. By the way, when are you going to come by the apartment?"

Nat had already asked me this several times this week. "I don't know. I don't want to intrude on the newlyweds."

She laughed. "Yeah, right. Ben works all night and is usually half dead when he comes home. And I'm usually pretty tired from being pregnant. The newlyweds are acting more like old fogies anyway. Trust me, we're not very exciting.

"Why don't you come over tonight?" she suggested suddenly. "Ben's working anyway. It'll be just you and me."

Since I couldn't think of an excuse, I agreed.

I spent most of a pretty boring evening in Nat and Ben's tiny, stuffy, barren apartment, and was I ever glad to get back home. Okay, the truth is their place reminds me of a prison cell. It's in an old complex downtown. It's run-down and looks like it might collapse at any minute. I'm surprised it's not condemned. Their unit is on the first floor, which might appeal to Nat since she doesn't have to go up the stairs, but the street is so noisy that I wonder how they can even sleep. The worst part is that there are bars on the windows.

"For security," Nat explained as she leaned back into the frumpy futon Ben had brought from home. She rubbed her hands over her ever growing belly in a circular motion, acting like it didn't even bother her that her jeans were unbuttoned and her T-shirt was rolling up.

"Right..." I said, glancing away.

The apartment has one miniature bedroom, which is mostly filled with Nat's full-sized bed from home, one creepy little bathroom that smells like mildew, and a boxlike kitchen that Nat has filled with her shower and wedding things. And then the "living" room that's not even as big as my bedroom. And that's it. Of course, they don't have much to put in it. But that's probably just as well since there's not much room anyway.

"Ben's mom is going to an estate sale this weekend,"

Nat told me. "She said she'll try to find us a table and chair set."

"Won't it be a little crowded in here when the baby comes?"

"Oh, we'll find a bigger and better place by then," she assured me.

"Oh, yeah."

I'm still not sure how we managed to pass nearly two hours, but finally I told her that I was pretty tired and made my escape. Poor Nat, I thought as I drove home, she can't escape.

But now I'm thinking maybe she really likes it. I mean, she actually seemed pretty okay. Maybe not happy exactly, but she wasn't depressed either. And then I remember how she was last summer, when I thought she was almost suicidal. I guess this is better than that. So who am I to judge? Maybe this whole marriage thing is really working for them. Just because it wouldn't work for me doesn't mean it's wrong for them. Even so, I know that I'm going to really be praying for them—praying that God will bring good out of what looks like a plain old mess.

Monday, October 16

The previous couple of weeks passed fairly quietly. Uneventfully even. And I think I kind of welcome the change of pace, not to mention the peace. Nat has started going to the pregnant school downtown. Okay, it has a name, but I just can't remember it. She wants me to come check it out, but I guess I'm not ready for that yet.

It feels like I've been trying to figure out my own life for a change. Like where do I fit in, who are my friends, what can I look forward to during my senior year? I'm even asking God to show me how He plans to use me this year. Okay, that's a new one for me. To be honest, I think I've been fairly self-absorbed in the past—asking God what He can do for me rather than what I can do for Him. I think I'm ready to take the next step. At least that's what I wrote in my prayer notebook yesterday.

And today I got a pleasant surprise. Maybe even an answer to prayer. Allie Curtis was back in school.

"What are you doing here?" I asked her as we stood in line in the cafeteria.

"Same as you." She grinned. "Finishing up my senior year."

"I thought you were done."

"No, that's just Chloe and Laura. I'm the one who got stuck behind."

So I filled her in a little on Nat and Ben and how I was feeling a little stuck behind too. "But I'm getting used to it," I said. "And it's kind of nice having a routine without all the drama and stuff."

She nodded. "Yeah, I can appreciate that."

As it turns out, Allie will be here until spring break. After that Redemption goes on tour again. Laura and Chloe will be taking classes at the community college, and the band plans to do a few benefit concerts in the area while they're here.

"The record company calls it a hiatus," Allie explained as she paid for her food. "But I think we just needed a little break."

"Is it hard being a celebrity?" I asked as we looked for a table.

She kind of laughed then shrugged. "It's got its ups and downs." She nodded toward a table to our right. "Want to go sit with Marissa and Spence?"

Okay, the truth was, I didn't really want to sit with those two. I mean, Marissa can be a real pain, and everyone knows Spencer is a doper. But since I had actually prayed about being used by God, and since I really did want to sit with Allie, I agreed. Before long, Cesar and Jake joined us. And things started to lighten up, and I got to thinking maybe it wasn't too bad after all. I know that as Christians we need to mix it up with people who aren't. That's something Chloe has always been good at. And it seems Allie gets this too.

"That was cool," I told Allie later as she and I walked out of the cafeteria.

"What?" she asked.

"Hanging with the riffraff."

Allie laughed. "You mean Spencer and Marissa?"

"Yeah. I hate to admit it, but those guys make me uncomfortable sometimes. I mean, I've tried being friends with Marissa, but it usually comes back to bite me."

"Chloe and I used to be the riffraff," Allie told me as

we walked to the senior locker hall. "So did Cesar and Jake."

I considered this. "Yeah, I guess you're right. We're all riffraff when you get right down to it."

Allie grinned. "We're all riffraff. I like that. I bet Chloe could turn that into a song."

"She's welcome to it," I said as I removed my violin case from my locker.

"I forgot about you and your violin," Allie said as she eyed my case. "You should come jam with us again. That was fun."

"Anytime," I told her. Then we parted ways. And for the first time since my senior year started a month and a half ago, I felt like maybe it wouldn't be a total wash after all. And maybe, just maybe, God was up to something.

Saturday, October 21

Youth group was very cool tonight. Both Allie and Chloe were there, along with Cesar and Jake, and even the newlyweds showed up. And though the group was relatively small, in some ways it was just like old times.

"Look around the room tonight," Josh said, after we started to settle down following a pretty loud worship time led by Chloe and Allie. He waited as we glanced around the group of familiar faces. "Tell me what's wrong with this picture," he finally said.

No one said anything, so Josh continued. "We need

to grow, both inwardly and outwardly. Our internal lives need to grow as lovers of Christ, and we need to grow outwardly as a group. We need to start reaching out to others, inviting kids into our world."

So this prompted a fairly lively discussion about whether or not we should invite unbelievers to youth group. Some of the kids felt that youth group should be a place for fellowship and learning. Others felt that it should be a place for outreach.

"So, what's the answer?" Josh asked.

"We need a place where we can come to get lifted up," said Kerry. "It's not easy being a Christian all week, hanging out with kids who don't exactly respect your opinions, you know."

"That's true," said Chloe. "And even though I'm not in high school anymore, I've felt pretty challenged at the community college lately. I mean, I'm used to everyone knowing I'm a Christian and being kind of, I guess, respected for my beliefs. But at college I'm a nobody, and when I get a chance to share my faith, it can get pretty gruesome." She smiled then. "Not that I don't enjoy getting beat up a little. I actually think God is teaching me some things through this. Still, it's so great to be here with a bunch of Christians who really get me. Kinda healing, you know? I wouldn't want to lose that."

"I know what you mean," Cesar said. "But I get what Josh is saying too. I can see the need to bring kids who don't know Christ to a place where they can be loved and accepted for who they are." He glanced at me now.

"Like having lunch with Spencer and Marissa, Kim. It was good seeing you around this week. It's been a while since you hung out with us."

I nodded. "I know. I think that's going to change." I looked back at Josh now. "And I totally get what you're saying about reaching out to others. In fact, I've been praying that God will show me how to do it. And I've been trying."

"So, it's like we need both," Josh said for clarification. "Any ideas how we can do that? Do we have two nights of youth group? One for bandaging up believers and one to bring others in to hear the Good News? Or what?"

Suddenly Chloe stood up. "I've got it!"

Everyone got quiet and looked at her.

"Sorry, I didn't mean to take center stage," she said to her brother.

He laughed. "Hey, this is an open discussion."

"Besides, we're used to it," quipped Allie.

"I want to hear what she's got to say," Caitlin said, leaning forward with interest.

"Okay." Chloe took a deep breath. "This is the thing... As you guys probably know, Mike Trapp owns the Paradiso. And I was talking to him today, and he told me how he and Jill want to move to Arizona to be close to Jill's mom since she's pretty sick. And he told me that he's going to sell the Paradiso. He jokingly suggested that Redemption should buy it and—"

"That's a great idea!" Allie said, standing now. "We've been looking for some investment opportunities!"

"Yeah," Chloe said, "and maybe we could use the coffeehouse for an outreach. Like make sure we've always got some Christian kids around to talk to other kids."

"And maybe you could have an open mike night," said Cesar. "Like Mike used to do. A way for kids to share their faith."

"And maybe you could sell Christian books and music," said Jake.

"We've got some direct outlets to that." Chloe winked at Allie.

"This is a very cool idea, Chloe," Josh said. "But before you commit to anything, you better put it all before God. You don't want to jump into something without His blessing."

"That's for sure," Chloe said. "And we need Laura's blessing too."

Everyone got pretty excited about this possibility, and we kicked around all kinds of ideas for how we could all help to make it work, including volunteering to work the counter and even sweep floors.

"Ben would be good at that," teased Nat. And although a few people laughed, Ben didn't look too pleased.

"We'll talk to Laura," Chloe finally said, "and get back to you."

"In the meantime, let's take a few minutes to lift this idea up to God," Josh proposed.

After youth group, we continued to talk about the

coffeehouse. Some started suggesting that we rename it—something that sounded "more Christian."

"No," said Chloe. "I think it's just right as it is. We don't want to make people uncomfortable being there."

"Besides," I said, "Paradiso means paradise. And that's exactly what the coffeehouse should feel like. Coming to a little paradise where God is present."

Chloe nodded. "Exactly!"

I felt excited as I drove home. Like I was actually going to participate in a mission of sorts. And now I've committed myself to really pray for this endeavor, that God will open all the right doors, and that our whole town will get blessed as a result.

Dear Jamie,

I'm sixteen and totally bored with my life. My parents tell me to "get involved" in something, but there's nothing I really want to do. I don't really like sports, music, drama, art, or anything to do with school. It's like I don't really want to do anything. Besides that, I don't have any friends. What's wrong with me?

Bored Girl

Dear BG,

Okay, my first reaction is that people who are bored are boring. And that might be why you don't have any friends. Your parents are right; you do need to get involved in something. But my second reaction is to wonder why you don't want to get involved. I'm guessing that 1) you're just lazy and sitting in front of the TV or computer too much, or 2) you may have really low self-esteem, or 3) maybe you're suffering from real depression. Only you can decide what the real reason is. But if it's not the first one, you may need to get help. Start by honestly talking to your parents or a counselor, telling them how you feel. Then you might need a complete check-up with your family doctor to determine the next steps. But you need to DO something. It's your life, and it's up to you to get in there and live it!

Just Jamie

Six

Friday, October 27

"It's a done deal," Allie told me this morning. "Redemption officially owns the Paradiso. We signed the papers last night."

"That's awesome!" I told her.

"Yeah, everyone agreed it was a good investment. Our lawyer even told us that we might consider making it a nonprofit to offset our earnings." She shrugged. "I don't really get how that works, but our parents seemed to think it was worth considering. The cool thing is that we get to take occupancy this weekend."

"Let me know if there's anything I can do to help," I said as we walked to the science department.

"Great," she said. "We're going to need it. We've got all kinds of ideas. But for starters, Chloe thinks we should have like a board of directors or something like that. A group of people who can help keep it going in a good direction while we're on the road, you know. And your name came up."

"Really?"

"Yeah. Chloe thinks pretty highly of you, Kim."

We parted ways then, but all morning long I kept thinking how cool it was that they would consider me to be on their board. That means a lot.

Allie caught up with me again on the way to lunch. "I forgot to tell you," she said. "We kind of want to keep it under wraps that Redemption is the new owner of the Paradiso."

"No problem." I didn't mention that I'm pretty good at keeping secrets.

"I mean, we know that word will leak out, but we just don't want to make a big deal of it. We want everyone to feel comfortable coming there—not like they're going to church, you know?"

"I totally get that," I told her as we got in the lunch line. "I remember how I felt before I gave my heart to the Lord. I wouldn't have been comfortable in a place that felt dominated by Christians." As I picked up a tray, I remembered how Natalie used to preach at me, how she used to try to get me to her church, how she wanted me to be "saved" and what a turnoff that was.

Hopefully we can protect the Paradiso from becoming like that. Funny how I'm already thinking "we" when it comes to this little business venture. You'd think

I was investing my own money. But maybe it's because I'm investing my heart.

Saturday, October 28

Laura came to youth group with Chloe and Allie tonight. And together, the three of them made the announcement about the Paradiso. They also made it clear that they wanted to keep this news as quiet as possible.

"It's not like people should care who owns it," Laura pointed out. "But it'd be cool if it didn't turn into the focus."

"And," continued Chloe, "we decided that although we want the youth group in Faith Fellowship involved, we need to make it open to other churches too. So we don't look exclusive. Although we do plan to keep a tight control over what can and cannot happen there."

"Yeah," said Allie. "We don't want kids showing up trying to get other kids saved. I mean, that's our goal, of course, but we don't want that attitude like 'I've got to get this kid saved so I can put another notch on my belt,' you know?"

"That's right," said Chloe. "It's more about making friends, loving people right where they are, showing them that Jesus accepts us as is. And that He's the one who does the changing." She looked at Caitlin now. "The way my sister-in-law reached out to me a long time ago."

Caitlin laughed. "Hey, I didn't even know what I was doing back then, Chloe."

"Well, God did, and that's how we want to treat others. Just by being their friend."

After that, Josh did a great study about the way Jesus reached out to sinners while they were still sinning. I was really glad I'd brought a notebook and was taking notes. I have a feeling it's something I'll be reviewing from time to time.

"So you see," he said in conclusion, "Jesus didn't tell those sinners to clean up their act and to call Him when they had it all together. Instead, Jesus in essence said, 'Let Me get to know you, and you get to know Me, and then let's see what happens next.' And, of course, all kinds of miracles happened after that."

Now as I sit here, writing in my diary, I'm thinking that being a Christian is really pretty exciting. I can't wait to see what God does next!

Tuesday, October 31

Tonight was the grand reopening of the Paradiso. Of course, no announcement about new ownership was made. But Redemption did run an ad in the paper announcing that they would be doing a few songs there on Halloween and also that there would be some special tricks and treats involved for anyone who came in costume.

And it was a totally cool night. The place was packed,

and Redemption's performance was really awesome. For the most part, they did songs with a gentle message. And finally Chloe did a solo with her acoustic guitar that went a little deeper. But not so much that it turned anyone off.

People in costume received a "treat" package that contained a free CD (that Redemption's recording company donated), along with a coupon for a free coffee (for another date) and candy. I was in charge of putting these together and didn't do a bad job if I do say so myself. Okay, I felt a little silly (at first) coming dressed like a black cat, but the idea was for me to stand at the door and give the packages away. After a while, I realized I was actually having fun.

People who weren't in costume got a few tricks. Like a fake coffee drink that wouldn't come out of the cup, or a can of those springy worms that was disguised as a to-go coffee cup. But people just laughed and had a good time.

I had hoped that Ben and Nat would come. She thought maybe he had the night off, but I didn't see them. They missed youth group last week too. And I realize now as I'm updating my diary that I haven't talked to Nat for more than a week. I hope everything's okay. I'll be sure to give her a call tomorrow.

Saturday, November 4

I called Nat today, and she did not sound like a happy camper. But, even so, she wouldn't reveal what was wrong. The more I pestered her, the quieter she got. And then finally she just started crying.

"I'm coming over," I tell her, not even waiting for her response. Then I hop in my Jeep and head downtown. And what I see when I get there is really unsettling. No, it's worse than unsettling. It's scary.

Nat does not look good when she opens the door. And it's obvious that she's been crying—a lot. The place is pretty much a mess, but worse than that, it stinks.

"What is that awful smell?" I ask her.

She points to the kitchen, where it looks like someone has been mopping the floor. "I was trying to clean it up, but it kept making me gag."

"The smell is making <u>me</u> gag." So I go over for a closer look and realize that someone has hurled all over their cruddy-looking linoleum floor. "Gross!" I say, almost stepping in it. "Are you having morning sickness again?"

She gets a funny look, as if considering this, but then just shakes her head. "Ben."

"Is Ben sick?"

She shrugs. "Yeah, sort of."

"Does he need to go to the doctor?"

She rolls her eyes. "Maybe to a shrink."

"Huh?"

Now Natalie goes over to the futon and sits down, and putting her head between her hands, she starts crying again. Well, that smell is just about making me want to lose my breakfast, so I pick up the mop and pour some more disinfectant into the bucket, and holding my breath, I start cleaning up the mess myself. When I finish, I take the mop and bucket and set them outside their front door. I just want to get that smell totally out of here.

Then I go and sit next to Nat. "What's going on?"

She looks up at me with red, swollen eyes, reminding me of the girl I put up with all last summer. "It's Ben."

I nod. "Yes. Ben threw up. But why?"

"He's been drinking."

"Drinking?" I actually blink at this news. "Are you sure?"

"Yes. He started drinking with some guys after work. He says it's how he relaxes."

"Seriously?" Now for some reason I have a hard time imagining Ben O'Conner drinking—let alone getting wasted, like it appears he must've done.

"Go look at him if you don't believe me."

So I decide to take her up on this and peek in the bedroom, where Ben is flopped across the bed, still dressed with shoes on, and looking pretty wiped out. I actually go over to see if he's still breathing, and he seems to be. It smells disgusting in here too, so I just close the door.

"This isn't good, Nat."

"Tell me about it."

"Does anyone know?"

"You mean besides his drinking buddies?"

"Yeah. I mean like Josh or Caitlin or his parents?"

She shakes her head. "No, of course not. Ben would freak if I told them."

"Have you told your mom?"

Her eyes open wide. "No way!"

Okay, maybe I can see her point. Mrs. McCabe would flip out and then be furious with both Ben and Nat. She was barely keeping it together at the wedding. Maybe it's better to leave her out of this.

"What are you going to do?" I ask.

"Do?"

"Yeah."

She just shrugs.

"You can't just let this go on. I mean it's definitely not good for Ben. It's not good for you either. And what about when the baby comes?"

"I know. That's what I keep telling him. But then he just gets really mad..." She looks down at her rounded stomach.

I think about this for a moment. It's just all so weird. Ben O'Conner drinking so much that he's drunk, vomiting on the floor, and then getting mad? "How mad?" I ask Nat in a quiet tone.

"Really, really angry." She looks up at me now. There are new tears in her eyes. "He says horrible things to me, Kim. I—I think he hates me." And then she loses it.

I put my arms around her and hold her while she cries really hard. All I can think is, why—why—why? Why did Nat allow herself to get to this place? Why is she staying here? It's obviously seriously messed up.

What's the point? Finally, she's pretty much stopped crying, and she leans back into the futon and wipes her nose on the sleeve of her fairly grimy looking sweatshirt.

"I know you think I'm pathetic, Kim." She looks down at her lap. "But I love him."

I don't say anything just yet. I'm trying to figure out what's best to say. Finally I pray silently, asking God to give me the right words. I've blown it with Nat enough times in the past to know that this situation is going to take something more.

"Nat..." I begin slowly, "I know you love Ben. But you can see that there's a problem here."

She nods.

"And I know you've been trying really hard to make things work. And you've had a good attitude and everything..."

"I'm trying."

"But maybe this thing—this marriage with Ben—maybe it just wasn't meant to be," I say.

She sits up straighter now. "We made our vows, Kim," she says in a firm voice. "We promised God and each other that we would stay together for better or worse, in sickness and in health, and I intend to keep that promise."

I nod, wondering how to possibly counter that. What would Jamie say? "But what if Ben can't keep those vows, Nat? What if he—"

"He has to keep those vows. He has to stick with me. I'm having his baby. We're a family." She's waving her hands for emphasis. "Yeah, I know it looks bad right now. We're just going through a rough period. It's hard on Ben. He's not used to working and going to school. And those guys he hangs with after work." She just shakes her head. "They're the worst. If he'd just lose the losers, everything would be fine."

I don't say anything.

"And, we need to get to church. We need to make it to youth group. Ben didn't work last Saturday, but he went out with his new buddies. I was too embarrassed to come by myself."

Now I hear a noise from the bedroom, and it sounds like Ben is waking up, and suddenly I feel totally weird being here. It's like I'm completely out of my realm, and I really don't know how to deal with this. "Nat, I love you, but something is really wrong here. And I'm worried about you. And Ben too." I stand up and move toward the door. "You guys need help."

"Do <u>not</u> tell anyone, Kim," she says, standing too.

"How can I not?"

"You're my best friend," she says with a creased brow. "And I never would've told you if I didn't think I could trust you. Ben and I are going to deal with this. And we don't need a bunch of people interfering."

"You guys need some kind of help."

"No, we're going to get through this, Kim. Pastor Tony told us during our premarital counseling that marriage isn't easy. He said it's something you have to work your way through, but that it's worth it."

"But, Nat—"

"No buts." She gives me that look now. The one I've only seen a few times from her, but it's to warn me not to step over the line. Our friendship is at stake.

"Okay." I give in.

Then she hugs me. "Thanks, Kim. It means a lot that you came over. I know I can trust you. And really, I think this was just a good wake-up call. Ben will probably be really sorry today. He'll probably realize that he needs to stop drinking and start acting more responsibly."

"I hope so." But even as I say this, I doubt it.

"Nat?" I hear Ben's voice.

"You better go," she says in a hushed tone.

And I don't argue with her. Feeling like I just stepped out of the twilight zone, I walk away from the apartment complex just as it starts to rain. And now as I sit here finishing today's entry in my diary, I think that as much as I love Nat, I am getting so tired of her life. God forgive me, but I am.

Dear Jamie,

My best friend's parents are really cool. And I love being at their house. It's like they're more like friends than parents. They just hang out with us and watch movies and stuff, and it's fun being with them. The only problem is that they think it's okay to drink alcohol, and they don't have a problem letting us kids drink with them. They say that it's better than doing it out on the street where someone could get hurt. And the only reason this is a problem is because my parents would kill me if they found out. I guess I'm starting to feel guilty about the whole thing. What should I do?

Confused

Dear Confused,

No wonder you're confused. This is not how responsible parents act. And I'm sure you know this or you wouldn't have written. Giving alcohol to minors isn't just reckless; it's illegal. And these "cool" parents could wind up in some real hot water. There are several things you could do. 1) You could confront the "cool" parents and tell them about your concern over this habit and that you won't be able to come to their house if it continues. Then stick to it. 2) You could tell your parents what's up and be ready for the fireworks and some restrictions. 3) You could anonymously report what's going on and just sit back and watch what happens. Or last of all, and your very worst option, 4) do nothing and wait until it all hits the fan and everyone gets in big trouble. Hopefully you won't do that.

Just Jamie

Seven

Saturday, November 11

I've talked to Nat twice this week. But only on the phone. Both times she just glossed over what happened last weekend. She told me everything was "fine." But without any details. It was the kind of reassurance that isn't reassuring at all. I know she's covering something up.

"Do you want me to stop by this morning?" I asked when I called to check on her. "I'm going over to the Paradiso anyway."

"No," she said sleepily. "I didn't sleep very well last night. I want to sleep in this morning."

"Is everything okay?"

"Everything's fine," she said in a somewhat snippy tone. "It's just the baby. I'm getting bigger, and I have to get up to use the bathroom all the time." She let out a moan. "Being pregnant is not fun, Kim."

"I didn't think it would be."

"I can't believe I still have almost two months before the baby is due. Getting up all night to use the bathroom, watching your body getting stretched out of shape... Well, it's not for the faint of heart."

"Maybe the getting-up-all-night thing is good," I said, looking for the positive side.

"What on earth for?"

"Maybe it's God's way of preparing you for when the baby is born. You'll have to get up all night to take care of it."

She let out another moan. "Ugh, I don't want to think about that."

"It's a fact of life, Nat."

"Did you just call me to torture me?"

"No, I just wanted to check on you."

"Well, you did, thank you very much."

"So what are you doing today?" I asked. And I was actually curious. I mean, I can't imagine what I would do if I was stuck in that little hole-in-the-wall apartment. It would be like being in prison.

"I don't know..."

"Why don't you come by the Paradiso," I said. "I'll spot you for a mocha—a decaf, of course."

"I don't know..."

"You haven't even been there since Redemption bought the place. They've made some pretty cool changes."

"I might come by..."

"Good. I'll be there until three."

"Okay, see ya later then."

Even as I hung up, I had my doubts as to whether I'd really see her there. And as it turned out, I didn't. And I didn't see her or Ben at youth group tonight. But that wasn't as surprising. I did, however, ask Cesar if he'd seen Ben.

"I've called him a lot," Cesar told me. "But it seems like he's always working. And so far he hasn't returned my calls."

I frowned.

"Is everything okay with them?"

I gave him my can't-talk-about-that look, remembering my promise to Nat.

Cesar sighed. "It wouldn't be surprising if they were having some problems. That's a lot to adjust to. I can't even imagine what I'd do if I was in Ben's shoes."

I laughed. "Well, that's something you'll never have to worry about."

He grinned. "See, there is an upside to kissing dating good-bye." Then he pointed at me. "I haven't seen you going out with anyone since your breakup with Matt."

I kind of shrugged. "It's not that I've kissed dating good-bye. It's more like I decided to take a break."

"Good for you."

"Yeah...I guess."

Now I'm back home and feeling worried about Nat. My theory is that she's avoiding everyone. I think she's embarrassed about the way she looks. She's getting really big now, and none of her clothes fit right, and for whatever reason (maybe money) she hasn't really gotten any maternity clothes. But besides that, I think she's depressed. She just doesn't seem like herself anymore. And if I had to bet, I'd say that it's probably because of Ben. Not that I'm blaming him completely. I mean, he's probably depressed too. He's just dealing with it differently.

It's too late to call Nat tonight, but I think maybe I'll call her tomorrow. I have an idea. Maybe I can take her to look for some maternity clothes. I just got a check for the syndication of my column, and it was a lot better than I expected it to be. I guess my dad's newspaper has sold it to some more papers. Anyway, Natalie has always loved going to the mall. Maybe I can cheer her up by helping her to get into some clothes that fit.

Thursday, November 16

Nat and I actually went shopping tonight. I'd been calling her all week, but she kept blowing me off with some really pathetic excuses until I finally pinned her down and she agreed to go. But as soon as I picked her up, I noticed that something seemed wrong. For one thing she was wearing a lot of eye makeup, which isn't really like her. But besides that, she kept giving me these odd little sideways glances. Pretty weird.

When we got inside the well-lit mall, I noticed that her left eye looked kind of strange. "What happened to your eye?" I asked as we walked to a store that specializes in both maternity and baby things.

She reached her hand up to touch it. "Oh, that...it was just really stupid. I was sweeping the kitchen last weekend, and I'd forgotten to close this cupboard door, and you know how cramped it is in there. Well, the next thing I knew, I smacked right into the door. Really hurt too."

"Yeah, I bet."

We went into the maternity shop and were pleased to find some things that looked like real clothes. "You could probably even wear this after the baby is born," I told her as I held up a T-shirt.

"That's the whole point," a saleswoman said with a smile. "Maternity clothes aren't just for being pregnant anymore. And it usually takes the little mother a few months to get her figure back."

"A few months?" Natalie looked shocked.

"Oh, about six usually. Some women snap back sooner."

"Well, that's what I plan to do." Nat held up a pair of low-waisted flared jeans. "These are pretty cute."

"Yes," said the woman, "and that panel at the waist is adjustable. It gets bigger and smaller to accommodate your ever-changing body. When is the baby due?"

"Early January."

"Oh, maybe it'll be a New Year's baby," the saleswoman said. "Did you know that the first baby born in a new year gets all kinds of special gifts?"

"I've never heard that," Nat said as she picked out another pair of jeans.

"Oh, yes." The woman nodded. "We even donate some things from our baby department. It's a pretty big deal."

"Guess I better have my baby on New Year's then." Nat winked at me. "I think I'll try these on."

I waited while Nat tried on several things, going back to find her different sizes until she finally picked out a pair of jeans and three tops.

"Are you sure, Kim?" she asked as we walked back to the saleswoman.

"I'm positive, Nat. I want to do this for you, okay?"

She smiled and I noticed that black eye again. And I'm sorry, but it didn't really look like something you could get from a cupboard door. But I didn't say anything.

"Want to look at baby things?" I asked after the woman handed Nat her bag.

Nat just shook her head. "Not really."

"Are you registered yet?" the woman asked.

"Registered?"

"For baby gifts." The woman smiled at me now. "For the baby shower, dear. Surely some of your friends will be giving you a baby shower."

Nat giggled. "Well, I don't know..."

"Why not register anyway?" said the woman. "Just in case."

So I walked through the store with Natalie, watching

as she checked boxes on the long registry form. I could only imagine what all that stuff would cost, especially since this store isn't exactly cheap. "Maybe you should register at places like Target too," I suggested.

She frowned. "Are you saying my baby's not worth the good stuff?"

"Not at all. But I happen to like Target."

"I guess it wouldn't hurt."

Of course, as we left the mall, I was plagued with guilt. I do not want to have another shower for Nat. It seems like I barely recovered from the last one. Maybe someone from church will do it. Or someone from Ben's family. Maybe even Caitlin!

Tuesday, November 21

I've been working part time at the Paradiso, and I really like it. For one thing, it gets me out of the house, but besides that, it's a great way to meet new people. And I'm finding out I actually like that.

"Want to jam with us on Saturday?" Chloe asked me tonight as I was wiping down the espresso machine just before closing.

"But I work."

"Not until the afternoon." She points to the schedule. "We can quit by noon."

"Sounds great!"

"And if we work something out, maybe you'll want to play with us during open mike too."

"That'd be awesome," I told her.

"Can I ask you something?" she said after the last couple left the coffeehouse.

"Sure." I rinsed the dishrag out in the sink and turned to look at her. I could tell by the tone of her voice that this was something serious. I hoped I hadn't done something wrong. I was usually very careful, but you never know.

"You and Nat are best friends," she began in a hesitant voice. "And I don't want to be nosy, but Caitlin's been really worried about Ben. It's like he's dropped off the face of the planet. And I realize he's working and they're newlyweds and stuff, but do you know how they're doing? Is everything okay?"

I took a deep breath and considered my answer.

"I wouldn't ask," she said quickly, "but Caitlin is such a good friend to me. And she's too nice to ask anyone herself. She keeps saying they probably need to give Ben space. But he hasn't talked to Josh or Cesar or anyone. And that just doesn't seem right to me."

I nodded. "Yeah, I can understand the concern."

"But if you can't tell me, I'll understand."

I pressed my lips together, trying to decide what to do. "Nat has told me not to tell anyone... But I will say this—there are some problems."

Chloe nodded. "That's understandable. I mean, seriously, what a hard way to start a marriage."

"It's been hard. On both of them, Chloe. And the truth is—I'm really worried about both of them. And without revealing too much, I think that Josh should go have a talk with Ben."

"Really?"

"Yeah. But I didn't tell you anything, did I?"

"No. Not really. But I'll tell Josh to give Ben a call."

"Not just a call," I said suddenly. "I mean Josh should make a point to actually see Ben. Even if he has to pop in at work, or at the apartment, or whatever." Okay, I knew I was starting to sound urgent then. But I really wanted someone else—someone besides me—to know what was going on.

And as I sit here writing this, I'm thinking that Nat's black eye wasn't from the cupboard. Ben had probably been drinking, gotten angry like Nat said he does sometimes, and hit her. And that just makes me sick. In fact, if Josh doesn't follow up on this, I think I will. I will ask Nat to tell me what's going on, and I will tell someone. Maybe not their parents. But I could tell Caitlin and Josh or Pastor Tony. They should know what to do.

Making this decision feels like a heavy load's been lifted from me. And before I go to bed tonight, I will really be praying for Nat and Ben. I'll be asking God to get them some real help.

Friday, November 24

This was our first Thanksgiving without Mom. And it was weird how it hit both Dad and me pretty hard. Earlier this week, Dad found out that ski season would open on

Thanksgiving Day, and he suggested we go on up there. At the time it sounded great. And maybe it was, but it was tough too.

The snow was fairly good, and it was awesome being on my snowboard again, but the slopes were conspicuously empty, and my guess was that everyone else was home having turkey with their families. I'm sure Dad felt this too. So instead of being a good distraction from what—rather who—we were missing, it felt as if our grief was in the spotlight. But we never mentioned this as we took advantage of the short lift lines, until the place finally started to close at four.

"I thought we could grab a bite to eat on our way home," Dad said as he stuck our equipment in the back of my Jeep. I'd offered to drive today, hoping this would be good practice for me and maybe Dad wouldn't worry so much if I came back up here again for snowboarding.

"Sounds good." I climbed in and started the ignition. We didn't talk much as I drove to the nearest town. And we quickly discovered that the only place open was a very nice restaurant, where they were serving a special Thanksgiving menu.

"Hey, we'll get our turkey, after all," I told Dad as we went inside.

But I could tell that he wasn't too happy with this. And finally, after the waiter brought our food, I had to ask him what was wrong.

"I'm sorry, Kimmy," he said sadly. "I was just remembering..."

"Mom?"

He nodded.

"I've been missing her too."

He nodded again.

"But we'll get through this." I tried to sound more hopeful than I felt at the moment.

"Yes. I know." But I could see his eyes glistening.

"I've heard that holidays are the worst," I said, a lump growing in my throat.

"Yes." Now he looked around the restaurant, as if taking it all in—the wood beams, the pine-paneled walls. Finally his gaze fixed on the large stone fireplace that was burning cheerfully. "This is where I brought your mother last New Year's Eve."

I stared at the fireplace. "Oh."

"She loved this place."

Now I looked back at his untouched food. "We can go, Dad," I said quickly. "I'm really not that hungry."

"No..." He shook his head and reached for his fork.

Then we both picked at our food in silence. And before I knew what hit me, tears were slipping down my cheeks.

"I'm sorry, Kim," he said when he noticed me blotting my eyes with my napkin. "I didn't mean to upset you too."

"No..." I waved my napkin at him. "It's not your fault, Dad. I just, you know, miss her—a lot. I mean, I was thinking about her pumpkin pie today. I don't like anyone else's pumpkin pie. And now we'll never have it again."

"Maybe you could make it," he suggested with a hopeful expression. "Use her recipe."

I nodded. "Yeah. Maybe."

"She'd like that, Kim."

"I know." I looked around the restaurant again. No wonder Mom loved this place. It was really pretty cool with the softly burning oil lamps and old pieces of art on the wall. "I think she's glad that we're eating here, Dad."

His eyes lit up a little. "I think you're right."

Finally, we'd eaten as much as we wanted, and the waiter came over. "We've got a really good pumpkin pie to go with the special," he told us with a bright smile.

But we both declined. My dad asked for the check, and I carefully drove us home. Happy Thanksgiving. Okay, I guess it could've been worse. The good thing is that it's over. One less holiday to get through this year.

Sunday, November 26

Yesterday was so cool. I jammed with Redemption. They're trying some new things, some quieter, mellower songs, and I actually worked pretty well with them. And so later that night, I joined them for an open mike performance, and it was so awesome. Okay, I know they won't be inviting me to join their band anytime soon, but it was pretty cool just the same.

Chloe didn't mention anything about Ben today. And I was sort of glad. I'm sure she passed along to her brother what I said by now. And hopefully he's on it. But to my disappointment, Ben and Nat weren't at church today. And when I called their apartment this afternoon, Nat sounded pretty gloomy. I really wanted to mention my conversation with Chloe to her but knew that would be a dead giveaway that I'd said something. Even if I didn't give any specifics. Instead, I just kept the conversation light and finally told Nat to call me if she needed to talk or anything.

"Thanks," she said as if she really meant it. "I really do appreciate you, Kim."

And, okay, that just broke my heart. I mean, I was thinking about poor Natalie living in that horrible little apartment, going to the pregnant girl school, putting up with Ben's anger and drinking binges—and was it possible that he was abusing her too? It just made me feel really sick.

I'd be tempted to go over there right now, but it's Ben's day off, and I can't stand the thought of seeing him face to face. I'm getting really mad at this guy. I'm thinking, grow up! I mean, sure, Ben never wanted this, but he made all the choices that landed him here. No one forced him to have sex with Nat. No one held a gun to his head to marry her. And I'm sorry, but if he's feeling trapped right now, well, it's a trap of his own making. Get over it, Benjamin O'Conner!

Dear Jamie,

Everyone in my family is fat. Both my parents and my sisters and even my little brother are all obese. I mean, really fat. Like together we might be a ton overweight, but I can't remember how big that is. The thing is, I don't want to be fat. But I feel trapped. I feel like no matter what I do, as long as I live in this house, I will continue to be fat. I really want to leave home. But I'm only fifteen, and I know I can't live on my own. What should I do?

Finished with Fat

Dear Finished,

The good news is that you want things to change. The bad news is that it's probably not likely that you can move out. But you can still take control of your life—and your weight. It's not that hard to lose weight, if you really want to, that is. Mostly it takes eating a sensible diet with things like fresh vegetables, fruits, whole grains, low fat proteins, combined with a lot of exercise—which can be as simple as just walking. I suggest you see your family doctor and get some professional advice about these things, and then stick to a program. Then let your family know you're serious about losing weight, and maybe they'll decide it's time for them to change their lifestyle as well.

Just Jamie

Eight

Saturday, December 2

I didn't have much success talking to Nat this week. It felt like she was trying to shut me out, acting like everything between her and Ben was perfectly fine and good and brushing off any questions that got too close.

And when I talked to her yesterday, she actually sounded pretty good. She told me how she and Ben had gone to his parents for Thanksgiving and how great it had been and how cool it was to be part of their family. "Josh and Caitlin were there too," she gushed. "And everyone is getting so excited about the baby. And it sounds like Caitlin is going to give me a baby shower."

Well, I must admit that's a relief.

So what was to prepare me for what happens today? On second thought, it might be better not to expect these kinds of things. Anyway, it starts off with a frantic phone call, early in the morning. My dad sleepily brings the phone to my room, telling me it's Natalie.

"Kim," she says in a frantic voice. "I need help!"

"What's wrong?"

"Can you come over?"

"I—uh—I guess."

"Right now?"

"I'm not even dressed."

"Please, Kim. I need you right now."

"What's wrong?" I ask again. "Is it the baby?"

"I'll tell you when you get here."

"Are you okay?"

"Just hurry."

So I'm feeling a little freaked as I pull on some clothes and rush through the house.

"Anything wrong?" my dad asks as he measures out the coffee.

"I don't know. Natalie sounds pretty upset."

"Is she having the baby?"

"I don't think so," I say as I dig in my bag for my keys. "She wouldn't say what was wrong. She just wanted me to come."

He frowns. "Hopefully she's just being dramatic."

"Hopefully," I say as I leave.

But as I drive downtown I feel fairly sure that she's not just being dramatic. And when I go into her apartment, it's obvious that something is wrong. Really wrong. Although there's no vomit on the floor this time, the place is a wreck, and I see what appear to be broken dishes swept into a pile in a corner and a broken chair that's sitting in a heap.

"What happened?" I ask in a voice that's much calmer than I feel.

"Ben flipped out." She's pacing back and forth in the tiny living room now, wringing her hands as tears pour down her face. "He was drunk—and—and he was being mean—and—and he told me he hated me and that he didn't want to be married and that he'd—he'd rather be dead."

"Oh, Nat." I go over and put my arms around her, and I'm amazed at how big her stomach has gotten. But she is shaking, and it feels like she's about to fall completely apart.

"I—I don't know what to do, Kim."

"Sit down," I tell her as I lead her to the futon, which is still in one piece. "Just sit here and try to breathe." Then I go to the kitchen, where the cupboard doors are hanging open, some by only one hinge, and I find a glass and fill it with water. Who knows why I do this? But I take it back and tell her to drink it slowly. And she does.

I glance toward the closed bedroom door. "Is Ben in there?"

She shakes her head and hands me back the glass. "He left."

"In his car?"

She shrugs.

"He was driving his car, Nat? Drunk?"

"I guess..."

This is not good. Nat is still shaking, and I'm afraid I'm not helping much. "Have you had anything to eat, Nat?"

She just gives me this blank look.

So I go back in the kitchen and pour her a glass of orange juice and bring it back. "Drink this. Remember it's not just you...it's the baby too."

So she drinks it, and I think maybe she's not shaking so much. But as I sit there, I do not know what to do. It's like I can't wrap my mind around this whole situation—a situation that I've felt was wrong from the get-go. Not that I'm glad to have been right about this. I would've much rather been wrong.

"I don't know what to do, Kim," she says again. "I've just been walking around the apartment for hours, trying to figure out what to do."

"And you didn't call your mom or anything?"

"How can I?"

I consider this. How can she not? I mean, it's not like she can hide this thing forever. "Why don't you go lie down, Nat. You and the baby could probably use some rest."

She starts to resist, but I take her by the hand, tugging her to her feet and finally walking her to the bedroom. It's not quite so messy in here. The bed is made, but I can tell someone has slept on top of it. I pull back the covers and help her to ease herself down then tuck her in. "Just rest. I'll start cleaning stuff up."

"Thanks, Kim..."

I close the door and go back out and look around. But instead of cleaning up, I step out the front door and turn on my cell phone. I call information and get Josh and Caitlin's number.

"Hello?" says Caitlin.

"Caitlin," I say in a shaky voice. "This is Kim Peterson and I'm with Natalie right now and—"

"Is she going into labor?"

"No, no..." I try to think how to put this. "It's not that...but there's a problem, a pretty big problem—with, uh, Ben and Nat. Do you think that you and Josh could come over to the apartment?"

"Of course. We'll be right there."

"Thanks."

I go back into the apartment and consider cleaning up the mess, but then I decide to wait. I want them to see this for what it is. Including the empty Jack Daniel's bottle still on the floor.

Josh and Caitlin get there about twenty minutes later, and I open the door and let them in. "Nat's asleep," I say in a quiet voice.

"What happened?" Josh asks as he sees the mess.

"Where's Ben?" asks Caitlin.

And so I try to tell them the story. I try not to make Ben sound too much like the devil.

"Oh my gosh!" Caitlin says as she sits down on the futon. "This is unbelievable."

"So you guys had no idea?"

"Cesar told me that Ben was dealing with something," admits Josh. "I met him for coffee one night, and it seemed like it was just regular newlywed stuff. Ben acted like things were okay, just a little rocky. I figured it was natural that he was struggling some. Getting married and becoming a parent..."

"And being only seventeen," adds Caitlin.

"I had no idea he's been drinking."

"Or abusive," says Caitlin. While pouring out my story, I had told them about Nat's black eye.

"I don't know that for sure," I say quickly. "It's just an assumption."

"It doesn't really matter," says Josh. "It's obvious that they're in trouble."

"I hope Ben's okay," says Caitlin.

"Why don't you try his cell?" suggests Josh.

So Caitlin goes into the kitchen and uses the phone.

"I didn't know who to call," I say lamely. "And it didn't seem right not to tell anyone. Although Nat's going to be really mad."

"You did the right thing, Kim."

"His phone's turned off," says Caitlin. I can see the worry in her eyes.

"He's probably sleeping it off somewhere," says Josh.

"Should we clean this up?" Caitlin looks around the apartment.

Josh nods. "That's probably a good place to start."

So we all start cleaning stuff up, and it actually doesn't take too long. We're just finishing up when

Natalie comes out of the bedroom. I can tell by the way she looks at me that she's angry. But then Josh and Caitlin both hug her and tell her that they're here to help, and I think I can see relief in her eyes.

"I had to call someone," I say. "And I knew you didn't want your mom to see this."

"It's okay," she says sadly.

"You're going to have to make some decisions," Caitlin tells Nat. "But you don't have to make them right now."

"That's right," agrees Josh.

"I want you to pack some things," continues Caitlin. "And then we're taking you home with us."

Natalie looks around the apartment. "But this is my home."

"No, it's not," I tell her. "This is not a home, Nat. This is a prison."

And then she starts to cry.

"I'm sorry, but it's the truth, Nat. This whole thing is like a prison."

"Come on," Caitlin urges her. "We'll help you to pack some things."

So the three of us go into the bedroom and gather up some of Nat's clothes and personal items, putting them into a duffle bag, and finally we're ready to go.

"Shouldn't I leave a note for Ben?" Nat says, holding on to the front doorknob.

"No," says Josh. "Might be a good way to make Ben think about some things. Besides, I'll be in touch with him. I'll let him know what's up."

I feel kind of at a loss as I watch the three of them drive away, like I'm no longer needed. And yet I'm relieved. Nat's in good hands now. Josh and Caitlin will help her to figure out what to do.

And yet when I get home and sit at my computer to work on some homework and end up writing in my diary instead, I'm still really worried about Nat. What's going to happen now?

Since I can't answer that, I decide to answer a letter for my column.

Dear Jamie,

I know your letters are for teenagers and I'm only ten, but I decided to write you anyway. My problem is that I really, really, really want a dog!!! But my mom won't let me have one. What can I do to make her see that I gotta get a dog?

Dogless Dog Lover

Dear DDL,

First you need to ask your mom what her reasons are for not letting you have a dog. And you need to respect those reasons, especially if she says your house is too small or someone in your family has allergies or owning a pet is too expensive. In that case, you might offer to walk neighborhood dogs or see if you can volunteer at the local animal shelter—and that way you can still spend time with dogs. But if your mom's reasons don't seem reasonable, you might try writing out a contract where you agree to take care of the dog all by yourself. And list all the things that are involved in owning a dog. You may even have to consider working to earn money to help with expenses. If she sees that you're willing to do all that, maybe she'll decide that you're old enough and responsible enough to own a dog.

Just Jamie

Nine

Friday, December 8

So much has happened this week...where do I begin? For starters, Nat and Ben appear to be history. Serious history. Oh, Nat still has her moments when she thinks they could get back together, but I keep reminding her of the facts and giving her small doses of reality—not to depress her, but just to keep her head in the present.

Caitlin and Josh and Mr. and Mrs. O'Conner confronted Ben in the apartment later that same day we moved Nat out. I guess Ben had a pretty bad hangover, which made it even easier for them to make their point. Kind of an intervention, really. And it sounds like they did it in love, which was better than I probably would've done. I seriously wanted to lay into that boy. But as Nat keeps reminding me, I need to forgive him. I'm amazed at how easily she can forgive him. What's up with that?

"It's partly my fault," she told me on Monday. It was the first night she came to stay at our house. Nat's mom is too angry to allow Nat to go home just yet—if ever. And maybe it's for the best. We've got plenty of room here, and Nat seems to appreciate it. I was surprised at how easily my dad handled it. He was like "no problem." I think he was actually relieved to have Nat come here since it turns out he's been as worried about her as anyone. And the funny thing is, Nat listens to him. He was even talking to her about how adoption was really a wonderful thing, and she didn't argue. Go figure!

Anyway, back to Nat and how she thinks the big blowup with Ben is partially her fault.

"I can see now that it was the marriage, the pregnancy, the responsibility that was making Ben crazy," she told me that night. "It's just too much for a guy his age to deal with."

I nodded, thinking, Yeah, duh, I tried to tell you that about a billion times. But I don't say this.

"Ben never would've started drinking if we hadn't gotten married," she said sadly. "Josh helped me understand that."

"It did seem pretty out of character for Ben," I admitted. "I could hardly believe it at first."

"Me too. And then I told myself it was just a one-time thing. But it happened again, and again, and again..."

"Do you think Ben's an alcoholic?" I asked.

"He's agreed to an outpatient rehab treatment

program. He'll get some counseling and report to a mentor and attend AA meetings for six months."

"Wow, Nat, that's a pretty big commitment."

"Yeah, his parents told him that was the only way they'd let him come back home."

"So he's back home?"

She nodded with a glum expression.

"I know this is really hard on you," I told her in my most compassionate voice. "But, in the long run, I think you'll see it's for the best."

She shrugs. "Maybe..."

"Caitlin told me that she thinks it might be a good thing you guys got married."

"Really?"

"Yeah. She said that it might've been the only way for you both to figure out that it wouldn't work. I mean, if you hadn't gone through all of that, you might still be thinking there was hope."

"I suppose..."

"I know that God can still bring something good out of this, Nat."

She sighed. "Maybe, but sometimes I feel like I'm sitting in the bottom of a great big hole, a hole that just keeps getting deeper."

And I can understand how she might feel that way, but I happen to think she's slowly climbing out of the hole. I mean, she's been functioning pretty well this week. She uses my mom's old car to drive herself to the pregnant school every morning. And then she comes home and helps out around the house.

She even watches Krissy and Micah for a couple of hours after school, which you'd think would please her mom, although Mrs. McCabe is still treating Nat like she's a good-for-nothing degenerate. It's like she hates her own daughter. And, okay, Nat's blown it, but shouldn't she be forgiven? Especially by her own mother? Her mother who claims to be a Christian? I just don't get that.

Wednesday, December 13

I think my dad is making some real headway with Nat. It's amazing how she will listen to him. I suppose it has to do with her "absent" father. I know she's been hungry for male attention. That's probably one of the reasons she glommed onto Ben last year. I think he was sort of a "daddy replacement" for her. Oh, I'd never say that to her. Or anyone for that matter. But it's safe in my diary. Anyway, tonight at dinner, which Nat made on her own, my dad surprises both of us by asking Nat what her plans are.

"Plans?" she says as she passes me the butter.

"For your future?" he persists. "And for your baby?"

"Oh..."

"Not that you're not welcome to stay here," he says. "At least until the baby is born. I can't really say what will happen after that. But what are you thinking?"

"I, uh, I don't really know." She frowns. "I thought I'd

have my diploma before Christmas break, but that doesn't look like it's going to happen now. All the stuff with Ben and everything, well, I missed quite a few classes this fall."

"You could come back to Harrison," I suggest.

"But she couldn't bring her baby with her," Dad reminds me. "They don't have childcare there."

"That's right." I glance at Nat. "So you'll stay at the pregnant school then?"

"It's not the pregnant school, Kim. I keep telling you it's the Margaret Allander Michner School."

"Yeah, yeah. So are you going to keep going there?"

She sighs loudly. "I don't know..."

"You don't have a lot of time to figure these things out," my dad says as he takes a second helping of mashed potatoes.

"I know. I mean my scholarship at the Michner school is only good until the end of this term. I don't even know if I could get another one. And I know my mom can't help me."

"And childcare is expensive," my dad points out. "Not only that, you have things like health insurance to consider—which makes me wonder, how do you plan to pay for your medical expenses when the baby is born?"

She shrugs. "I guess I thought Ben's parents would help out. And I've heard that hospitals will sometimes forgive your debt if you're really poor." She kind of laughs, but her eyes look really sad. "And that pretty much describes me. Poor and homeless."

Okay, now I'm starting to get a little irritated at my dad. It's one thing for him to get her to think about her future, but it's another thing to make her feel like such a pathetic loser. I'm about to say something when my dad reveals where he's actually going with this conversation.

"You know, Natalie, there are lots of really good people out there who want to adopt babies. People who would cover all your expenses and even help you get back on your feet again. People who would love a baby and give it everything it needs." He turns and smiles at me. "There are people who would gladly take a child into their hearts and their homes and never, not for a minute, consider this child anything but their own."

Except for the ticking of the clock, the room is silent now. And I'm looking down at my plate, afraid to look at Nat, afraid that she will get really angry now. The way she gets angry at me if I suggest this, which I haven't for quite some time. I'm actually praying now, silently begging God to show Nat what's best for her life. I admit that I don't really know. It's just hard to believe, especially after all she's been through, that she will be happy being a single mother.

"I—I wouldn't even know where to begin," she says in a quiet voice. "I mean, how do you look into something like that? Who do you call?"

"I'm sure there are people at your school with connections," my dad tells her. "And even the agency that helped us find Kim deals with domestic adoptions."

"Domestic?"

"Within our country," he explains.

"Right." She nods as if she knew this. "Well, I guess I could talk to someone there. I mean, just to find out about it. I'm not saying that's what I'm going to do. But I suppose I could at least look into it."

My dad smiles. "That would be wise, Natalie. And I'm not trying to influence you one way or the other. I just think you need to take a really good look at what you're getting yourself into. No matter which way you choose."

"I know..."

"And your due date's only three weeks away," I remind her. "And babies can sometimes come early. What if you went into labor, like, tomorrow? What would you do?"

Now this really seems to get her attention. She looks seriously worried.

"See my point?"

She nods. "So if I make an appointment, would you be willing to come with me, Kim?"

"Sure. I could even say hi to some of my old friends."

"Old friends?"

"The people who helped with my adoption. My parents and I used to go visit them about once a year. They'd have this big party for international adoptees, and they'd take pictures and have cake and stuff. But we haven't been for a few years."

Dad smiles. "Kim thought she was getting too old for it."

"But I'd still like to go in and say hi. And I'm happy to go, Nat. But you better hurry and make that appointment."

Friday, December 15

I was feeling pretty freaked all day today. Nat's appointment at the adoption agency was at four o'clock this afternoon. And I knew it could go either way.

Thankfully she didn't back out of it. Even so, I prayed as I drove her over to the agency, and I held my breath as I parked the car. But to my relief she got out. To start with, I took her around and introduced her to the people I knew. Then we went into Helen Stein's office to discuss the pros and cons of adoption. And I have to give it to Mrs. Stein—she didn't pressure Natalie at all. She was actually very gracious and honest and helpful.

"With your due date so close, you really haven't given yourself a lot of time to make this decision," Mrs. Stein said finally, and I could tell she was wrapping up the appointment.

"I know." Nat frowned. "That's pretty dumb on my part."

"Don't be hard on yourself," Mrs. Stein told her. "It's a tough decision, and lots of young women put it off. The only problem is that if you don't make a decision and the baby comes—because babies are like that, they come when they want—then it becomes even more difficult. I'd be disingenuous if I didn't tell you that it's very difficult to hold your own baby in your arms and then hand it to someone else. It might be the most challenging thing a woman ever does. But, on the other hand, the longer you keep the baby, the harder it becomes. For everyone."

"Can I ask you a few more questions?" Nat said suddenly. "Or is our appointment over and you need to do something else?"

"You were my last appointment today," she tells her. "Go ahead. Ask away."

So Nat proceeded to quiz her more thoroughly on the difference between open and closed adoption, asking some very intelligent and well-thought-out questions. I was impressed.

"I don't think I'd want an open adoption," she said finally. "I don't think it's fair to the child."

Mrs. Stein nodded. "Some people feel that way."

"Like Kim here." She pointed to me. "If her birth mother had been in the picture, well, I think it would've been hard on your family. Don't you?"

"Yeah, I do. I mean, there was a time when I really wanted to find my birth mom. Remember how I searched and searched? And then when Mom got sick last year, I remember thinking that she was my <u>real</u> mom and why would I even care to know my birth mother?"

"But we do have ways of allowing kids to contact

their birth mothers," Mrs. Stein pointed out. "We draw up papers before the child is even born stating exactly what both sets of parents want. For instance, later on down the line some teenagers have a need to meet their birth parents, and if everyone is agreeable and it's permissible according to the contract, we arrange for this to happen. But some people want their privacy protected, and we ensure that this happens as well. Each adoption is as individual as the child and the parents involved."

"Is there anything I should fill out?" Nat asked. "I mean, like an application or something?"

Mrs. Stein nodded. "There's a lot of paperwork." She turned around and pulled a folder from the shelf behind her. "It's not quite as bad as buying a house, but it does take some time."

"May I have that?"

Mrs. Stein slid the folder across her desk. "Does this mean you're interested, Natalie?" The woman looked as surprised as I felt. Was it possible that Nat was serious?

"I—I—think so."

"And you understand that the birth father must sign off as well?"

Nat rolled her eyes. "That shouldn't be a problem."

Mrs. Stein smiled. "You are going to be making someone very, very happy, Natalie."

I controlled myself from applauding or even patting her on the back.

Natalie frowned. "And even though I want the closed adoption, is there any way I can find out something about the parents? Can I meet them?"

"Just about anything is possible. You're calling the shots, Natalie."

"I just need to know they're good—really good people—" Nat's voice cracked just then. "That my baby will be loved and well cared for."

"We have a very thorough screening process," Mrs. Stein assured her. "Besides things like police checks, we do random home checks, talk to neighbors, friends, relatives. We're very, very careful."

Natalie nodded. "Good."

"I think you'll see that the paperwork is fairly self-explanatory, but if you have any questions, please feel free to call." Then she handed Nat a business card. "This even has my cell phone number if you need to call over the weekend."

Then Nat thanked her, and we walked out. I couldn't believe it. Nat sounded like she was seriously thinking about this.

"Do you think it's the right thing to do?" Nat asked as she slowly climbed into the Jeep. She's so huge now that it's not easy for her to get in and out of anything.

"I really do, Nat." I put my key in the ignition. "But it's your decision. You're the only one who really knows what's best for you."

"Me and God, you mean."

I smiled at her. "Yeah. That's what I meant."

She started filling out the paperwork as soon as we got home. I've pretty much stayed out of her hair, not wanting to distract her. And I've heard her ask my dad to explain some things to her. And he's actually been very helpful. I think Nat's baby is going to find a good home!

Dear Jamie,

I'm sixteen and I have finally fallen in love. "John" and I have been dating since October, and he is so perfect for me. I've gone out with other guys, but John is different. He likes to talk, and he listens to me and respects me and everything. I am so lucky!!! I know you get asked this a lot, because I've been reading your column for a year, but I really think that John is the ONE. And he's asked me (not pressured me) about sex. He's a senior, and he's never had sex before either. What would be wrong with having sex? Especially since I know he's the one, and I know that we'll get married someday. Why not?

Lucky in Love

Dear LIL,

"John" does sound like a good guy. And you definitely sound in love. But I don't think that means you're ready for sex. Here are my reasons: 1) Having sex outside of marriage can ruin what sounds like an otherwise good relationship. It messes with your emotions and sets you up for ultimate heartbreak. 2) Having sex outside of marriage, at your age, almost <u>*never*</u> *leads to marriage. Just the opposite. And it creates obstacles to future relationships with guys.*

3) Having sex outside of marriage can lead to sexually transmitted diseases. (How do you know for absolute certain that he's never slept with anyone?) 4) Having sex can lead to pregnancy—are you ready to have a baby?

Just Jamie

Ten

Monday, December 18

Nat and I went to meet with Mrs. Stein again. Nat turned in her paperwork with everything filled in except for Ben's signature.

"I left a message for him," Nat explained, "telling him to call you and come in and sign the papers. I don't really want to see him."

"No problem."

"I wanted to talk to you about the adoptive parents now," Nat told her. "If you don't mind."

"Not at all."

"Well, when I filled in the form about what kind of parents I wanted for my baby, I wasn't sure about the age. I wrote that I wanted them to be young. And that's so that they can be active and play with the child and stuff. But then I got to thinking about Kim's parents, and they were older, but they were also really great parents. And my parents were young, and they ended up getting divorced...so I just wasn't sure."

"Don't worry, Nat," she assured her. "None of our parents are terribly young. We require that they be married for at least seven years. So even if you said you wanted 'young' parents, they would have to be old enough to fit our requirements. Does that make sense?"

She nodded. "Definitely. I just thought I'd clear that up."

"And did you take the doctor's form to your obstetrician?"

"Yeah. They said they'd get it back to you by the end of the week."

"Great."

"So that's it?"

"Unless you have any other questions."

"Well, that booklet pretty much explained what happens when the baby is born. But I guess I'm still curious. Am I supposed to talk to the adoptive parents? I know that I won't know their names or anything, but I'd kind of like to just talk to them. Really briefly, you know."

"That's not a problem. The adoptive parents will be coming from out of state, and I'm sure they'd like to meet you as well."

"Good."

"So how are you feeling?" she asked Nat.

"Big and fat."

Mrs. Stein laughed. "That'll change soon."

"And I keep having these Braxton Hicks contractions. They're driving me nuts."

"That's just your body's way of getting in shape so you'll be ready for labor."

"I know. But I'm ready already."

"Have you taken the hospital's childbirth class yet?"

Nat frowned. "Ben and I had signed up to take it last month. But we never made it."

"Don't they have that class every Tuesday night?" Mrs. Stein asked.

"I guess."

"I could go with you, Nat," I offered.

"Really?" She looked at me. "You'd be willing to be my labor coach?"

"Labor coach?"

"That means you stay with Nat when she's having the baby. You go into the delivery room with her," Mrs. Stein explained. "You help her with breathing and give her ice chips and just general encouragement. Are you good with that sort of thing?"

"I don't know..."

"She used to be a real wimp when it came to hospital stuff," Natalie told her, then turned to me. "But you've changed a lot, Kim. I think going through the thing with your mom, well, that's made you a lot tougher. Don't you think?"

I nodded. "I guess."

"So would you be willing to be Natalie's labor coach?" Mrs. Stein asked. "It's a pretty big commitment."

"Don't do it if you don't want to," said Nat.

"Yes," agreed Mrs. Stein. "I'm sure we can find someone around here who would be willing. My assistant, Jessie, has done it several times."

"No..." I said slowly, considering my response even as I answered. "I think I'd like to do it." I smiled at Nat. "I mean, we've already been through so much together. Why back out now?"

"Good." Mrs. Stein actually clapped her hands. "That's excellent."

Tuesday, December 19

So it is that I find myself in a meeting room at the hospital with a bunch of pregnant women. And oh yeah, some husbands and "partners" too. A midwife named Ramona teaches this class. She looks like a real earth muffin to me, with her long braided hair, baggy clothes, and funky shoes. In fact, she reminds me of my cousin Maya, which reminds me I haven't heard from her in at least a month. Maybe no news is good news.

Ramona gives us some reading materials as well as some general tips about things like breathing, timing contractions, and keeping the mother-to-be relaxed and happy. Then we take a quick tour of the hospital, primarily the labor and delivery section. We're also shown the patient admittance area, cafeteria, and emergency entrance. "In case you go into labor after midnight," Ramona explains.

Then we're taken back to the original room, where we are shown a film of a real birth. Now, okay, I'm trying to be a good sport here, but I'm sorry, that film just totally freaks me. I actually closed my eyes during a couple of scenes. I cannot believe I signed on for this. I'm wondering if there's any way to back out. Oh, I probably won't. Not really. But I'm not looking forward to this. Not one little bit.

Friday, December 22

Christmas (or winter) break officially began today. And not a moment too soon either. As much as I like school, I am so ready for some downtime. All this stuff with Nat, combined with writing my column, helping out at the Paradiso, and keeping up with homework, not to mention violin practice, is starting to wear on me. I was looking forward to just hanging out on the home front. And maybe I'd even put up some Christmas decorations or try out some of Mom's Christmas recipes.

I tried to talk Nat into going to the youth group's annual Christmas party with me last night, but she wouldn't even consider it.

"It'll be fun, Nat. And you've been stuck in the house all day."

"Yeah, like I want to show up looking big as a cow so that everyone can get a good laugh at my expense. Think again, Kim."

"They wouldn't do that. They're Christians and they—"

"Christians can be some of the meanest," she says, shaking her head. "Trust me, I know this to be true."

I have a feeling she's talking about her mom. But I also remember a time when Nat was pretty vicious to me for dating Matt last year. Of course, I know better than to remind her. She's miserable enough as it is.

Finally, I'm about to leave, and Nat, looking frighteningly like a beached whale, is flopped out on the leather couch, remote in hand, and staring glassy-eyed at the TV. It's a good thing my dad's at his grief group tonight, because I'm pretty sure he would not appreciate this image in his family room.

"Sure you won't change your mind?"

She just rolls her eyes. "Forget it, Kim. I'm not moving."

Okay, I do feel a little guilty as I leave, especially since I'm leaving her all alone, but not guilty enough to stay home. And it's not that I can't see her point. I'm sure if I were in her shoes—or pink bunny slippers, as is the case tonight—I'd be keeping a low profile too. (Although that metaphor doesn't work so well for someone in Nat's condition.)

Also, I realize as I drive to church, it's possible that Ben could be there tonight. Okay, it's not likely. But I saw Chloe today at the Paradiso, and she told me that Josh is keeping pretty close tabs on Ben, making sure that boy sticks to his rehab agreement as well as going to church regularly. Even so, I seriously doubt that Ben will be showing his face around youth group anytime soon.

I'm surprised at how many cars are in the parking lot. And the party looks pretty packed. When I go in I notice some new faces, which I think might have to do with our clandestine outreach ministry at the Paradiso. Allie and I made sure to invite Marissa and Spencer tonight, although I would be shocked to see either of them. Redemption is going to do some music, and Spencer admitted that their little "girl band" is pretty impressive. So who knows?

I mix and mingle with friends and am having a pretty good time, when my cell phone rings. I didn't even know it was on. I answer it but can hardly hear over the noise. Finally, I go outside to hear better.

"Kim!" Nat is screaming. "It's time! I'm in labor! Get home now!"

My hands are shaking, and I'm trying to think. "But that'll take too long," I say. "Why don't I just meet you at the hospital?"

"You want me to drive?" she yells.

"Call your mom. Have her drive you."

Now the line is so quiet that I think I've lost my connection or maybe she's passed out from the pain. "NAT! Are you there?"

"I can't call my mom," she sobs. "You're my coach, Kim. Please, I need you."

"Fine. Just be ready, okay. I'll be there in about twenty minutes. Hopefully I won't get a ticket. And—" I suddenly remember—"don't forget to call your doctor."

"I already did. Drive fast, Kim."

But as soon as I hang up, I know this is totally crazy. Nat's mom could easily get her to the hospital in fifteen minutes, and I could be there waiting for her. Otherwise it could take us nearly an hour by the time I go all the way home and then back to the hospital.

I dial Nat's home phone number, the first number besides my own that I ever memorized, and wait as it rings. I hope this isn't a mistake.

"Hello?"

"Mrs. McCabe?" I say just as I approach the intersection where I'll have to either go home or head for the hospital. "Natalie's in labor. But she's alone at my house. I just left the church and could meet her at the hospital if you could pick her up and bring—"

"I'm heading out the door right now," Mrs. McCabe yells into the phone. "Krissy, Micah, move it. Your sister's having a baby!"

"Meet you there," I say, then hang up. Okay, Nat's going to kill me. But hey, she'll be so distracted giving birth that she'll probably forget all about this.

I get to the hospital and am just waiting at admittance when I see Mrs. McCabe pushing Nat in a wheelchair with Krissy and Micah trailing just a few feet behind. They have on their pajamas, but they're grinning like this is as much fun as going to the circus. And it starts to feel like a circus once Nat's in the hospital bed.

Between the nurses, who are hooking Nat up to some kind of monitor and taking her temperature, and Krissy, who's climbing on the bed and trying to "talk to" the baby, and Micah, who's turned on the TV, and Nat's mom, who keeps asking where the doctor is, I'm not sure who should be doing what. Finally, Natalie settles it.

"Kim is my labor coach," she tells her mom in a firm voice. "She'll be in the room with me."

Mrs. McCabe looks hurt, but what can I do? It's Nat who's having this baby. She should call the shots.

"Fine," her mother says in a stiff tone. "We'll be in the waiting room. That is, unless you'd prefer us to go home."

Nat is holding on to her stomach now. "I don't care what you do! Can someone give me something to stop this pain?"

I get some ice chips and try to remember how the breathing technique is supposed to work. Finally it feels like we get into some kind of a rhythm. I watch the monitor, which the nurse has explained to me, and when it starts to look like a contraction is coming, I tell Nat to start breathing. The only problem is that the contractions are kind of irregular. Some are five minutes apart and then Nat goes almost a half hour with nothing. Finally, it's nearly midnight, and I'm exhausted while Nat's actually asleep.

"How are we doing?" the doctor comes in and asks.

"I don't know," I admit. "I was about to ask you the same thing."

"Well, I'm afraid Natalie's experiencing some false labor."

Nat opens her eyes. "False labor?"

He nods. "It's fairly common."

"But the pain was real," she protests. "How can it be false?"

"It's a bit like those Braxton Hicks you've been having. Nature's way of getting you ready to give birth."

"But I am ready," she insists.

"But the baby isn't."

"How can that be?"

He smiles. "It's just one of those mysteries of life, Natalie. The baby comes when the baby is ready. And the baby is not ready to come tonight."

"But when?" she demands with tears in her eyes. "I can't stand to go on like this? When?"

"Well, it could be as soon as tomorrow," he tells her.

"Then why don't I just stay here?"

"Or it could be on your due date," he looks at her chart. "January 2."

She groans.

"Or it could be even later than that."

She leans back into the pillow and closes her eyes.

"I've told the nurses to release you, Natalie. You go home and get some good rest, and who knows? Maybe I'll see you back here tomorrow."

Okay, as I go to tell Nat's mom the news, I'm thinking that I'm with Nat. I want her to just have this baby and get it over with! I'm not sure I can do this all over again.

"False labor?" Mrs. McCabe frowns. "I should've known."

"Why?"

"Oh, this is so like her. Always the drama queen. I don't know why I fall for it." She turns and looks over to where Krissy is asleep on a couch. "Micah," she calls. "Tell your sister to wake up. We're going home."

"What about the baby?" Krissy asks sleepily.

"Not tonight," I tell her.

"You'll get Nat home just fine, I'm sure," Mrs. McCabe says to me.

And, of course, I do. But to be perfectly honest, part of me is beginning to resent the role that's being forced on me by Nat. And I am beginning to resent Nat's mother too.

"I'm sorry," Nat says when we pull into the driveway. "You must be totally sick of me."

"No," I tell her as I open the door. "But I am tired."

Even so, I go around and open her door and help her out of the Jeep. "Let's just leave your bag in the Jeep," I say as we go inside. "Just in case you go into real labor."

I'm relieved to see that Dad has gone to bed. I called him earlier to let him know what was up and then again when we found out it was a false alarm.

"I'm afraid I won't know the difference," she says as we walk through the kitchen.

"The difference?" I'm foggy now. What were we talking about?

"Between real and false labor."

"Like your doctor told you," I say. "The contractions need to be at least five minutes apart, consistently, for at least an hour."

"Or my water breaks."

"Yeah. And unless either of those things happens, don't call me," I tell her as I head for my room. "I'll call you."

"Sorry," she says again, standing in front of the guest room door.

"It wasn't your fault."

"Was my mom mad?"

I consider this. I could lie to her and say, "No, she was just fine." Instead I just nod.

"It figures." Then she shakes her finger at me. "I told you not to call her."

"Whatever..."

"Sorry," she says, looking down at her enormous belly. "I'm really thankful for you, Kim. You and your dad have been just like family."

Then I go over and give her a hug. "You are family, Nat. Now get some rest. Like the doc said, you could be having that baby tomorrow."

"Oh, I hope so!"

I don't tell her that I hope not. I'm not ready for a repeat of tonight just yet. I'm thinking I'd be just as happy to have her wait until January for the baby. Maybe it'll even be late.

Speaking of late, I really need to do another letter for my column.

Dear Jamie,

I am so depressed. I totally hate Christmastime. Nothing good ever comes out of it. I never get what I want. My family usually gets in a big old fight. It's just such a complete waste of time and money. I wish that someone would just cancel it for good.

Scrooge

Dear Scrooge,

I don't think you really get Christmas. It's not supposed to be about getting what you want or having good things happen to you. If you really want to have a good Christmas, why don't you look into some ways to help others? Find someone who's got it worse than you, and lend a hand. Maybe you'll discover that it's not about what you get, but what you give.

Just Jamie

Eleven

Saturday, December 23

Nat is in a black mood today. Really dark. I've tried to get her out of it. I baked cookies and put up some of Mom's old Christmas decorations. I even played some Christmas music, some of the funky old vinyl albums that my mom used to love. I thought our house was actually feeling pretty festive too, but nothing seems to bring Nat out of her gloom. This morning I even made us waffles for breakfast, the kind you make with batter and a waffle iron. But do you think that cheered Nat up? Think again.

"I'm going to be pregnant forever," she complained as I cleaned up my waffle mess. "It's God's punishment on me."

"Yeah, right." I put a bowl in the dishwasher. "That sounds like something God would do, Nat."

So then she pulled her sweatshirt up, revealing this enormous stomach with all these weird little purple lines running every which way, kind of like a road map. "Look at me, Kim! I'm gross and ugly and there's no way my body will ever be the same again."

Okay, I'm pretty shocked at the size of her stomach, not to mention all those lines, which I assume are stretch marks because she's been complaining about that a lot. And I guess I can almost believe her. I mean, how is it possible that her body ever will be the same? But for her sake, I tried to act like it's no big deal. "Look at the bright side. If God really is punishing you and you really are going to be pregnant for the rest of your life, you'll probably become famous. You'll be written up in the 'Guinness Book of World Records.' I'll bet Oprah will even want you on her show."

That's when Nat threw a potholder at me. Oh well.

And I'm not stupid. I'm well aware that she has plenty to be miserable about. I can't even imagine how I'd feel if I was her. I think I might rather be dead. And I know I should be more compassionate and kind, but after attempting to humor her all day yesterday and then again this morning, I needed a break.

"I need to do some Christmas shopping," I told her, knowing full well that nothing short of going into labor would tear her away from this house. I also knew that the mall would be packed and that I totally hate fighting the crowds. But I felt like it was simply the lesser of two evils. My mom used to say that.

"But, Kim—"

"Don't worry. I'll have my cell phone with me and turned on, and if you have even just one contraction, you can call me. Remember what the doctor said—it'll take an hour of contractions that are five minutes apart. And the mall's only twenty minutes from here. You'll be fine, Nat."

Of course, she didn't look fine when I left the house. She looked like she wanted to kill me. But seriously, what good would it do for me to stick around? I think we both need a little space right now. And the idea of going through my entire Christmas break with Nat acting like this—well, it's a little overwhelming.

The sad thing was, after I finished my fairly minimal Christmas shopping, which only included getting something for Dad and Nat, I still didn't want to go home. I double-checked my phone to see if perhaps I'd missed a call, but everything looked fine. So I decided to go over to the Paradiso, wishing I was scheduled to work and hoping that perhaps they'd be crunched and I could just step in and stay busy.

But it was pretty quiet over there, just a few customers, and Cesar was working behind the counter. "What are you doing here?" I asked him.

"Helping out," he told me.

"Where's Chloe?"

"Didn't you hear?"

"What?"

"Redemption has to do a Christmas concert in

Nashville tonight. All the guys in Iron Cross came down with the flu, so the recording studio had the girls flown out last night. Very last minute."

I sat on a stool at the counter and sighed. "What a cool life."

He laughed. "They weren't that pleased."

"Can you imagine?" I said to Cesar as he wiped the counter in front of me. "How awesome would it be to get on a plane, fly first class, get picked up at the airport by a limo, be taken to a really great hotel, and then you put on some glamorous costume to go out on a stage and perform in front of thousands of adoring fans?"

"Maybe you should ask the girls to give you the real story, Kim. I don't think it's quite as glamorous as you think."

"More glamorous than taking your best friend to the hospital and then finding out that she's not really in labor."

He gave me a sympathetic look. "I heard about that. If it makes you feel any better, Pastor Tony had us all pray for you."

"That's nice. It was about three in the morning when we finally got to bed." I held up my cell phone. "This is like our umbilical cord now."

"So, what can I get you?" he asked. "Something to calm your nerves? A nice gentle green tea, perhaps?"

I kind of laughed. "No, I think I need the hard stuff. I'll have a mocha with the works. And make it a triple shot."

His brows lifted. "Whoa, you really must be having a tough time."

I glanced around the coffeehouse, noticing that everyone was fairly far away from us and involved in their own conversations. And that's when I decided to unload on him. And Cesar, being Cesar, was big enough to take it.

"You're going to get through this, Kim," he said as he put my mocha in front of me. "And God is going to make you a bigger person because of it."

I frowned. "What if I don't want to be bigger? What if I just want a break?"

"Maybe we could help out," he suggested. "Kids from the youth group could take turns coming to visit Nat."

"Like babysitting?"

"More like an encouragement team. And a chance for you to have a break."

"So that maybe I could go snowboarding?" I said wistfully.

"Yeah, why not? You should get to have some fun during Christmas break. In fact, I wouldn't mind going myself."

"Maybe we could go together?" I said. "If someone else was willing to stay with Nat for a whole day." Then I shook my head. "No, it's not going to work."

"Why?"

"Nat would never agree to something like this."

"Why not?"

"She doesn't want anyone to see her right now. That's why she won't go to youth group or church or anything. It's like she's in hiding. Right now, all she wants is to have the baby, get back into shape, and hopefully resume some kind of normal life. I think she's hoping that everyone will just forget that any of this happened."

"But it would be good for her to be around other people," he insisted. "It'd help her to see that we still care about her, that we don't look down on her, and that she still has friends. You know?"

"I know. And you know. But convincing Nat of this...well, trust me, it won't be easy."

"That's okay. It's still worth a try. And you could use a break. Why don't you let me see what we can do? I doubt that we can get much together before Christmas, but Josh and I meet Monday morning. I'll mention this to him."

"Do you guys meet every Monday morning?"

"Yeah. He's kind of mentoring me. And then I'll do the same thing with another guy."

"Cool."

He nodded. "Very cool. I heard Caitlin is going to start doing it too. You should talk to her."

Then some new customers came in, and feeling somewhat cheered, I decided it was probably time to go home and check on Natalie. But when I got here she was taking a nap. So I tiptoed into my room and decided to just enjoy the peace and quiet.

Sunday, December 24

Today was pretty quiet. Nat said she wasn't feeling too well, so I went to church by myself. And she spent most of the day in her room. I'm sure it's because she was depressed. I tried to give her space, keeping myself busy by going to the grocery store, then putting together some things I thought my dad might appreciate. But Nat's laying low routine was starting to get to me. Finally I knocked on her door with a plan.

"Are you okay?"

"Yeah, just peachy." She rolled her eyes and patted her huge belly. "For a beached whale, that is."

"I know it's only Dad and you and me for Christmas Eve tonight," I told her. "But I'm trying to fix things like my mom used to do. She always made lots of finger foods and desserts and stuff. And sometimes friends would drop in, although that won't be the case tonight. Anyway, I thought it would be really simple to do this, but there's a lot more work than I realized. Can you help me out a little? I mean, you can sit down while you do it, but I thought maybe you could peel and cut up the veggies."

She pulled herself to a seated position with a loud groan, then glanced down at her frumpy pajamas, which looked like they could use a serious laundering. "Give me a minute to put on some decent clothes—that is, if I can find anything that will fit me."

"Thanks!"

So after a few minutes, Nat came down wearing her

snug maternity jeans and an oversized sweatshirt that my dad gave her, and I put her to work at the kitchen table. And although I really probably could've finished things off myself, I was actually pretty grateful for her company.

"I guess Mom and the kids have already taken off..." she said as she started to peel a carrot.

"I noticed them getting into their car around noon."

"At least I don't have to go through the traditional extended family feud this year."

I laughed. "There's something to be thankful for."

"Yeah, I guess." She picked up another carrot and sighed.

"But you still miss your family, don't you?"

"Kinda."

"Well, I kinda know how you feel."

She looked up at me then. "Oh, Kim, I totally forgot. I mean, this is the first Christmas without your mom. Are you doing okay?"

Her sympathy almost made me want to cry. Instead I just nodded, swallowing against the lump in my throat.

She shook her head. "Man, I've been so self-centered lately, acting like I'm the only one with problems. I'm sorry."

"It's okay. I mean, I realize that you're in a pretty hard place."

"Isn't it weird?" She held the peeler in the air as if to make a point. "I mean just last year, everything was so totally different. Isn't it freaky how things can change in such a short time?"

"I wonder how things will be for us next year..."

"You'll probably be off to some great Ivy League school. Maybe even where Matt's going."

"No thanks. I'm not applying there." I arranged my cheese slices on the platter, carefully fanning out the layers until they looked just right. My mom had a real knack for this, and my goal was for Dad to come home and feel like some things haven't changed.

"I wonder where I'll be..."

I didn't know how to respond to that. I mean, I know Nat still has options, but I'm not really sure what they are anymore. Her life has been so derailed these last nine months. And right now I think we're both so focused on her having this baby that we can't really see past it. I decided to change the subject by telling her about Redemption's Christmas concert. "They were supposed to get back home this morning. I hope it went okay."

"Did I tell you that Josh called yesterday? While you were gone?"

"No. What did he want?" I stopped what I was doing.

"He told me that it might be possible for Ben and me to get an annulment."

"An annulment?"

"Yeah..." She was looking down at the table now.

"Really?" I was trying to understand this. "Is that really possible?"

She didn't say anything.

"Well, that'd be cool," I said quickly, feeling bad for

doubting this. "I mean, that's like you guys were never even married then, right?"

"Do you want to know something, Kim?"

"What?"

"Well, it's about Ben and me, and it's kinda embarrassing."

Okay, now I wasn't so sure that I really did want to know. But at the same time, I could tell that she had something she needed to say, something she wanted to get off her chest. So I just nodded and braced myself.

"Ben and I never had sex after we got married."

I stared at her. "Never?"

She just shook her head.

"Not even on your honeymoon?"

"Nope."

"Why?" Now, I'm not even sure why I asked this because part of me really didn't want to know, but I guess another part was curious. And after all, she was the one to bring it up.

"I just didn't feel right about it that first night. I mean, being pregnant and everything—it just seemed kind of scary, and I was uncomfortable with the whole idea. Plus I was pretty exhausted after the wedding. I was so relieved when Ben agreed with me. And he said he didn't want to hurt the baby, which I actually thought was sweet. We said we'd get a book or talk to the doctor or something. But we kind of put it off. And then he started working those late nights, and we had school and stuff, and I was tired a lot, and then he started drinking and we started fighting. And I guess sex just became less and less appealing to both of us."

"Seriously?"

"Yeah. Do you think that's weird?"

I shrugged, feeling slightly uncomfortable, like I didn't really want to think about the fact that my best friend is married and that she's telling me this stuff. "I don't know, Nat," I finally said, hoping that I could be somewhat comforting. "Maybe it was just natural to feel like that. I mean you guys had been through so much. Maybe it was...oh, I don't know..."

"I think another part of it was that I was totally embarrassed for him to see me," she continued. "I was already getting pretty big, and I didn't feel the least bit attractive."

I nodded, pretending that I understood how she felt. But I really wanted to change the subject.

"The good news is that Ben told Josh everything...and because of that, well, we might be able to get a real annulment. And then we won't have to go through a divorce."

"That is good news, Nat." I smiled at her. "A nice Christmas present, huh?"

"Yeah, I guess. But it's kind of embarrassing too."

"Embarrassing?"

"It makes me feel so stupid for going through with the wedding and the bridal shower and everything, and then we're not even actually married. Do you think we should return the gifts?"

I kind of laughed. "Yeah, like everyone is going to want all those broken dishes and the used stuff back."

Nat started to cry. And I set down the ham that I was slicing and went over to her. "I'm sorry, Nat." I patted her back in an attempt to soothe her. "I was just trying to be funny. Of course, you shouldn't return the gifts. And you shouldn't feel embarrassed about the wedding and everything. You were doing what you thought was right. And like Caitlin said, maybe you guys had to go through that just so you would know that getting married was not the solution to all your problems."

"But I feel like such an idiot. And I'm sure that people are thinking terrible things about me and Ben. Like we're such a mess."

"The people who came to the wedding and the shower all love you, Nat. And I know they all just want the best for you. And I'm guessing they're all feeling relieved that you and Ben figured out what's best for everyone—and they should be thankful that you guys can get an annulment."

She looked up with wet eyes. "Really? You think so?"

"I really do."

"I'm not so sure about my mom though." Nat shook her head. "She'll think that she wasted her money on a sham wedding."

"She'll get over it."

"Do you know that I haven't even told her that I'm not going to keep my baby?"

"You guys really need to talk."

"It's hard to talk when she refuses to listen."

"Maybe after the holidays..."

Dad was pleased when he got home. "Kim!" he exclaimed when he saw my little feast spread out on the dining room table, just like my mom used to do. "This looks fantastic. Are we having guests?"

I shook my head. "No, it's just the three of us."

"Well, that's just perfect."

"Nat helped me do this," I told him.

"Thanks, Natalie," he said as he dipped a tortilla chip in the seven-layer dip, which I happen to know is his favorite.

I'd already put the Christmas music on and lit some candles, and I'd plugged in the lights on the little tree Dad and I had put up last weekend. Oh, the place wasn't nearly as festive as it was last year when Mom went all out, but it wasn't half bad either.

Dad wanted to watch our old "White Christmas" video, and Nat and I didn't argue. Afterward, Dad asked if we wanted him to do his traditional Christmas reading.

"What's that?" Nat asked.

"He reads this story about the first Christmas," I explained. "He's been doing it since I can remember. And I'm definitely up for it."

"Me too," said Nat.

So we listened while Dad read from my old picture book, but by the time he finished, Nat was crying—rather loudly.

"Are you okay?" I asked.

"I was just thinking about—about Mary," she said between sobs.

I nodded. "Yeah, I'm sure you can relate."

"But I was thinking about how—how horrible it must've been for her to ride on that donkey. I think I'd be dead if I had to do that."

Dad laughed. "Mary must've been made of tough stuff."

"And God must've helped her," I said.

"I feel so bad for complaining all the time," Nat said now. "You guys must be totally sick of me. And you've been so good to me, and I go around the place just moping and feeling sorry for myself." She held her chin up. "Well, I'm not going to do that anymore. From now on, I'm going to have a positive attitude. Even if this baby doesn't come until the middle of January." She made a face like she sure hoped that wouldn't be the case. "Anyway, no more pity parties for me."

"Good for you," Dad told her.

"I know I'll appreciate it," I said, gently nudging her and smiling.

It was getting late and Dad excused himself. "Sorry to be a party pooper, but it's been a long day."

"We'll try to keep it down in here," I joked.

"Merry Christmas," he told us as he shuffled off to bed.

Then Nat and I decided to watch "How the Grinch Stole Christmas," but it wasn't long before Nat fell asleep on the couch, and I wasn't that into the movie, so I decided to come up to my room.

I don't know why I'm not sleepy tonight. And even after writing in my diary, I'm still wide awake. I'd really like to play my violin, but I don't want to disturb anyone. Maybe tomorrow. I sit at my desk for a while, just looking at my mom's photo and missing her. I'm sure Christmas in heaven must be really special. But I wonder if she misses us. Or maybe she's watching. Finally, I decide to answer some letters, hoping that Just Ask Jamie will help put me to sleep.

Dear Jamie,

I think my dad's cheating on my mom. My best friend was driving us to the mall, and I noticed my dad's car at the intersection. He didn't see me, but I saw that he was with a lady from his work, and then he pulled into this sleazy motel and parked there. I want to tell my mom, but I know it's going to hurt her. What should I do?

Unfortunate Observer

Dear UO,

First of all, you need to tell your dad what you saw that day. Don't be confrontational about it, but do be direct and honest. It's possible that there's a perfectly logical explanation for what you saw. Maybe he was dropping the woman off for some reason. Or maybe you're right—maybe he is having an affair. How he reacts and the way he answers your question will probably tip you off. And if you feel certain that he is having an affair, you should tell him that he needs to tell your mom. So that you don't have to. Hopefully it'll turn out that he's not having an affair. But if he is, hang in there. Your mom will need your support.

Just Jamie

Twelve

Christmas Day

This has been one of the longest days of my life. And I am so thankful that it's nearly over. I think I will sleep for a week.

It all started shortly after I finally went to bed last night. I was just starting to drift off when I heard this quiet tap-tap-tap on my door.

"Kim?" calls Nat's voice as she cracks open my door. "Are you asleep?"

I sit up. "Not now."

"Sorry." She comes in and sits on the edge of my bed. "But I'm having contractions."

"What kind of contractions?" I ask, trying to sound more patient than I'm feeling. I'm just not up for another case of false labor tonight.

"I'm not sure..."

"Well, how many have you had?"

"It started about eleven," she says.

I glance at my clock to see that it's 11:37. "So, about half an hour?"

"Yeah, I think."

"How far apart are they?"

"I'm not sure. The first two were about ten minutes apart. And then the next one was a little less and—" She stops talking now and grabs her stomach. "And here comes another one." She reaches for my hand and puts it on her belly, which feels very tight.

"Can you feel that?"

"I guess." I turn on the light and just look at her. I can tell by her face that she's not comfortable. But even so, I'm not convinced this is the real thing.

"Why don't you lie down—" I move over and make room for her—"and we can time the contractions and decide whether or not you're really in labor. Okay?" She waits about a minute or so, then takes a deep breath and lies down beside me. "Okay."

I'm just about asleep when she's nudging me.

"Here's another one."

"Huh?"

"A contraction," she says somewhat impatiently.

"Oh yeah." I look at the clock and see that it's 11:48 now. "That's more than ten minutes," I tell her, closing my eyes again. I can hear her breathing, and I know that whatever's going on doesn't feel good. But according to the doctor, ten minutes apart isn't anything to be concerned about. Besides, I'm tired. I close my eyes and actually fall asleep. But it seems like only seconds have elapsed when Nat is poking me again.

"What?" I say in a grumpy voice.

"This is the real thing," she says. And I can see that she's standing next to my bed now.

I sit up and blink and look at my clock. It's 2:36. Even in my sleepy state I can do the math. "Nat!" I don't bother to hide my impatience now. "It's been like three hours since your last contract—"

"No, Kim," she says in an equally aggravated voice. "It's been like five minutes. My contractions have been exactly five minutes apart since 1:25. That's more than an hour. This is the real deal!"

"Are you sure?"

"I am in labor, Kim! And unless you want me to have this baby in your bed, I suggest you get up and get me to the hospital."

So I get up and pull on some clothes and then go to my dad's room. Within ten minutes the three of us are on our way to the hospital. My dad drives my mom's old car while I sit with Nat in the backseat and help her do her breathing techniques as I time her contractions. They seem to be getting closer, and I am getting really nervous.

"Hurry, Dad!" I urge him, knowing full well that he's going as fast as safely possible.

"I am, Kim. It's only five minutes away now."

Then Nat lets out a scream, and I don't know what

to do. Fortunately, my dad must have nerves of steel because he stays on the road.

"Hang on, Nat," I tell her. "We're almost there."

"This hurts, Kim!"

"I know, I know. But we'll be there soon."

It seems like days before Dad finally pulls up to the emergency room entrance. "I'll get someone to help," he yells as he jumps out of the car.

"Here comes another one!" Nat howls.

"Just breathe," I tell her in my calmest voice. And I do the breaths with her, panting like a dog just like the birthing coach in the movie did. "Come on," I urge her when I can tell she's holding her breath. "You have to breathe."

"You breathe!" she screams at me as my dad returns with a wheelchair and what appears to be a medical person. "Even better yet," she yells as they begin to extract her from the backseat, "you have this baby!"

I kind of laugh as I grab Nat's bag, and my dad and the medical guy ease Nat into the wheelchair. "She's not feeling so good right now," I tell the guy.

"Don't worry," he tells Nat as he wheels her in. "They'll get you as comfortable as possible as soon as you sign in." I run ahead and give the receptionist Nat's name and social security number, and she quickly locates her file. Soon a maternity nurse arrives, and it's not long before Nat's wearing her ID bracelet and being whisked toward the elevators.

"Call Mrs. Stein," Nat says suddenly. "She said to call

her as soon as I go into labor. The card's in my bag."

So watching them get into the elevator, I quickly locate the business card, dial the number, and leave a message. Then I catch the next elevator up, and just as I reach the maternity ward, I hear Nat yelling and follow the sound of her voice to a room. The nurse is trying to help Nat into the bed, but it's obvious she's having another strong contraction, and she's screaming so loudly that my dad bolts past me and makes an amazing disappearing act. I wish I could go with him. Instead I do the pant-pant breathing with Nat until the contraction finally ends, and then the nurse and I get Nat into bed.

Another nurse appears and starts hooking her up to the monitor and inserting an IV while the original nurse checks her vital signs. And by the time they're done, Nat's having another contraction. They seem to be coming about three and a half minutes apart now, and I'm hoping this means it won't be long.

It feels like several days before the doctor finally arrives and checks on Nat. "She's definitely in labor," he tells us with a big grin. "It'll be the first Christmas baby this year. And at this rate she'll probably deliver in a couple of hours."

"A couple of hours?" I say, thinking that sounds like years.

"That's not so bad," he tells me. "Most first-timers have a longer labor than that."

But then Nat has another contraction, and my

attention is diverted back to her and the breathing.

"I'll get her something to take the edge off the pain," he says as he writes something down on her chart.

"The sooner the better," I tell him between pants.

In between contractions, I feed Nat ice chips, wipe her forehead with a wet cloth, and try to be encouraging. "You're doing a good job. It won't be long now."

It's 4:25 when the nurse puts something in her IV. "That should help with the pain," she tells Nat. But it's too late; Nat's already having another contraction. The medicine takes about fifteen minutes to kick in, and things quiet down some after that.

Finally it's nearly six in the morning, and I am so exhausted I can hardly see straight. My throat is so dry from all this breathing and panting that I've been eating ice chips too. Why did I ever agree to do this? It seems like Nat is never going to have this baby.

"Pray for me," Nat says suddenly. "Please, Kim. Pray that I won't die."

"You're not going to die, Nat."

"Please!"

So I pray for her. I pray that God will get her safely through this ordeal and that the baby will be born whole and healthy. "And soon!" I say loudly. "Please, dear God, help this baby to be born soon!"

But shortly after that, things really start to change. Within minutes the doctor and nurse are agreeing that it's time for her to go to delivery, and Nat is lifted from the bed to a stretcher and being wheeled down the hall. The whole time she clings to my hand, and I jog to keep up with them.

"Don't leave me, Kim," she says in a hoarse voice. "Don't leave me!"

I stand at the head of her bed and tell her that she can do this. I breathe with her as she has contractions. But I don't look below her waist. I have no desire to see the actual birth. The fact that I'm here right now and haven't passed out yet is slightly miraculous.

The doctor tells her to push, then tells her to wait, then tells her to push, and I wish he'd just make up his mind. And finally, after what feels like years, the baby is born at 6:43 a.m.

"It's a girl!" the nurse informs us.

"A healthy, beautiful girl," the doctor adds, and then we hear a loud cry.

"You did it!" I tell Natalie. That's when I notice tears are streaming down my face. We're both crying now, and we hug and cry some more. After a few minutes the nurse brings the baby over for us to see. She now has a tiny pink cap on her head and is wrapped in a matching blanket.

"Eight pounds, five ounces," the nurse says. "Quite a big girl."

"She looks tiny to me," I say as I study the wrinkly red face.

"She's really okay?" Nat asks with a frown.

"She's perfect," the doctor says.

"Do you want to hold her?" the nurse asks.

Nat looks unsure. "Uh, yeah, I guess so."

The nurse hands Nat the baby, and I just watch. I'm trying to figure out how Natalie feels right now. Oh, I know she's relieved that the baby's born and that she's healthy. But how does Nat feel knowing that she's the mother of this tiny miracle?

Because that's how it seems to me. Like a real miracle. Like how does God do that? How does He make a perfect human being, tucked inside someone else's body? And then, just like that (okay not quite as easy as that), suddenly this miniature person is in this world and about to live her very own life. It's really amazing!

"Look at her fingers," Nat says with wonder. "They're so perfect. Even the tiny little fingernails." Nat pushes the hat up just a little. "And her hair. It's so soft and wispy."

"And blond," I add. "Like yours."

"And her eyes are so blue," Nat observes. "Look at how she's looking at me. It's like she knows me."

"She recognizes your voice," the nurse tells her. "Babies can hear before they're born, you know."

Now I'm getting worried. Where is Mrs. Stein? What if Nat suddenly changes her mind? What if she falls in love with this baby? What if she wants to keep her and raise her herself?

"We need to get you both cleaned up now," the nurse tells Nat as she holds her hands out for the baby.

"Good-bye, little baby," Nat says in a quiet voice, and I see that there are fresh tears in her eyes.

"We'll take good care of her for you," the nurse promises.

"Thanks." Nat hands the baby back.

"And after we clean you up, you can get some real rest," the nurse says. "And even have something to eat."

"Sounds good." Nat sighs.

"You did really great today, Nat," I tell her. "I was impressed."

"Did you call my mom?" Nat says suddenly.

I shake my head. "No, I don't know the number where they're staying."

"Get a pen." Then Nat rattles off the number, and I write it on my palm.

"Should I go call now?"

She nods and then leans back, letting out a big sigh. "Thanks, Kim. I couldn't have done it without you."

I kind of laugh. "Yeah, right. I'm pretty sure that baby would've been born no matter what."

"You know what I mean. Thanks. I don't know what I would've done if you hadn't been here for me. I owe you big time. If you ever have a baby, you'll have to let me pay you back."

Now I really laugh. "After watching you here today...well, I'm not sure I ever want to go through that."

"It wasn't that bad." She smiles now.

"Not that bad? Did you hear yourself screaming?"

"Oh, you know me—the drama queen."

"Yeah, right." I roll my eyes at her. "Get some rest,

and I'll go tell my dad the good news and call your mom. Maybe I should try Mrs. Stein again too."

"Yeah, thanks."

I tell Dad and he looks greatly relieved.

"I need to call Nat's mom," I say with a frown.

"You want me to call her?"

"Would you?"

"Certainly." Then he gives me a big hug. "You've been through enough for one day."

So he calls Nat's mom and I call Mrs. Stein. And to my relief, she answers.

"I got your message, Kim. How's it going?"

"She had a baby girl. Eight pounds, five ounces. She was born at 6:43, and she's perfectly healthy."

"That's wonderful! And how's Natalie?"

"She's okay."

"The adoptive parents are on their way to the airport right now. They expect to arrive by two this afternoon. Tell Natalie that she's just given a very nice couple the most wonderful Christmas present imaginable."

"That's right," I say. "I almost forgot it was Christmas. It seems like that was days ago."

"I'll be over to check on Natalie and the baby later this morning, and then I'll come again with the adoptive parents."

I hang up, but my dad is still on his cell phone with Nat's mom. I don't mean to eavesdrop, but it's not like I can help it.

"Natalie's been through a lot," he's saying patiently.

"We all have. Whether or not you come today or tomorrow is entirely up to you. But if she were my daughter, wild horses couldn't keep me away." Dad gives me a look, like he doesn't understand this woman or her way of thinking.

"Good," he finally says. "I'm sure Natalie will be happy to see you." Then he says good-bye and hangs up.

"Thanks for doing that."

"No problem. I just don't understand why Mrs. McCabe is having such a hard time with this."

"Are you forgetting how you almost had a heart attack when you thought that pregnancy test was for me last summer?"

"Well..." He grins a little sheepishly. "I would've gotten over it, eventually."

"Don't worry. After seeing what I saw today, I don't think I ever want to have a baby."

"Oh, Kim." His face is a mixture of relief and disappointment. "I'm sure you'll change your mind someday. Someday when the timing is right."

And now that this never-ending Christmas Day is almost over, I admit that I'm sure I'll change my mind someday too. Just the memory of that tiny little human—the miracle of that baby—makes me think I'd like to experience it too. But not for a long, long time.

Nat really liked the adoptive couple. Mrs. Stein had already told her that they were in their mid-thirties, had been married for twelve years, were college-educated, and both had good careers. Although the woman would be taking at least a year off, and after that she planned to work from home.

"As you all know, we don't disclose last names," Mrs. Stein said as she introduced Nat to the adoptive parents. "But this is Debbie and Mark."

"You've made this our best Christmas ever," Mark told Nat.

"The baby is absolutely beautiful," said Debbie. "I think she looks a lot like you."

"Her dad's pretty good-looking too," I added. Who knows why?

"You've made us so happy," said Mark. "You have no idea."

"We'll do everything to make her happy too," promised Debbie. "We'll love her and care for her like she's a little princess."

Nat smiled. "That's good to know."

"She's definitely going to be our little princess." Mark put his arm around his wife and gave her a squeeze. "We've waited a long time for this."

They talked for about half an hour, and then there seemed to be nothing left to say.

"Do you want to tell her good-bye?" Mrs. Stein asked Nat.

Nat's eyes filled with tears as she considered this, and everyone in the room waited in silence. I had no idea which way this was going to go.

"No," she finally said. "I held her this morning, and I said my good-byes then. I think it's for the best."

Nat and I didn't talk about the baby again for the rest of the day. Okay, it was kind of weird, but it just seemed the best way to go. I mean, what could I say? I know Nat was hurting. I know that giving up your child cannot be easy. Like Mrs. Stein said, it might be the hardest thing a woman ever does. And I know it was tough on Nat. And I have a feeling it's not over yet.

As it turned out, Nat's mom never did show up today. That made me really mad, and I might even give that woman a piece of my mind when she gets home. I know it hurt Nat deeply. Even my dad was upset.

"She didn't even get here in time to see her own granddaughter," he said when he picked me up from the hospital this evening. Nat is spending the night.

"Maybe it's for the best," I told him. But even now I'm not so sure.

Dear Jamie,

My grandma died a couple of weeks ago. But I keep thinking about her and crying a lot. I really miss her. Everyone else says that she's happy in heaven and I should get over this. But it's like I can't. So now I just make sure that no one sees me when I'm crying. Do you think I'll ever feel better?

In Pain

Dear In Pain,

Everyone grieves differently. Some get over losing loved ones quickly. Some never get over it completely.

The upside is that you must've had a good relationship with your grandmother. But this makes you miss her even more. Ask yourself these questions: How would your grandmother want you to deal with her death? Would it make her happy to see you in so much pain? Do you think she likes to know you're suffering? Or would she want you to remember the good times you had with her and to get on with your life and be happy again? And if that doesn't work and you're still deeply grieving and depressed, you might need to seek out the advice of a counselor or join a grief therapy group to help you get through this.

Just Jamie

Thirteen

Thursday, December 28

Nat came home from the hospital on Wednesday, and even though I can tell she's feeling bummed, she's doing a brave job of acting like everything's okay.

"Your family's home," I told her this morning. "I saw your mom's car in the driveway."

She just nodded, then took a sip of coffee.

"Do you think your mom will come over to talk to you?"

She shrugged. "I doubt it."

"Don't you think she'll want to know how it went? I mean, Dad didn't even tell her about the adoption. Do you think she'll be shocked?"

"I really don't know."

"Do you want me to talk to her for you?"

She seemed to consider this. "I'm not sure..."

"Because I really wouldn't mind giving that woman a piece of my mind."

Nat kind of smiled. "Yeah, I can just imagine that."

"She's your mother, Nat." I refilled my coffee cup and sat across from Natalie.

"I think she has disowned me."

"Well, that's just wrong." I set my cup down with a thud. "And I wish you'd let me go over and talk to her. I seriously think I might be able to straighten her out."

"Or just make her really mad."

I sighed. "Yeah, you could be right."

"But if you really want to..." Nat shrugged. "Well, go ahead. I guess I'd like her to know how things are, you know. Just to take a load off her mind."

I stared at Nat. "You want to take a load off her mind?"

"Yeah. I've put her through a lot. And I'm sorry."

"And she should forgive you," I persisted.

"You can't really force it."

"I know..."

"She'll come around in time, Kim."

"Well, how about if I just go over there and let her know that you're okay and about the baby and stuff."

She nodded now. "Yeah, I guess that'd be good."

So, telling myself that I would do this in a mature manner, I trooped over to Natalie's house. But before I knocked on the door, I shot up a quick prayer. I asked God to help me use the right words. It wouldn't really help anything if I blew up at her.

"Kim?" Mrs. McCabe looked surprised to see me. "What are you doing here?"

"Do you have a few minutes to talk?"

She opened the door wider. "Sure. Come in. Is everything okay?"

I walked in and stood in the foyer, considering my answer. "Well, that's why I'm here."

"Is something wrong?" Her eyes looked worried.

I nodded with a grim expression.

"What?" she said in an urgent tone. "Is Natalie okay?"

"She's okay in some ways. But in other ways, she's hurting."

"Oh." Mrs. McCabe seemed to relax now. "That's to be expected."

"Do you ever plan to talk to her again? Do you care about how she's doing? Or about the baby?"

"Come in and sit down," she said as she walked into the living room. I could hear the TV playing in the family room. I imagined Krissy and Micah sitting glued to the screen watching cartoons. She sat on the couch and motioned for me to do the same. "I know you care about Natalie, Kim. And you've been a good friend to her. Far better than she deserves."

"How can you say that? She's your daughter. Don't you want the best for her?"

"The best?" She leaned her head back and looked up at the ceiling. "Of course, I did want the best for her. I wanted her to live her life for the Lord. To keep her promise and to abstain from sex before marriage. And then I wanted her to marry a Christian man." She laughed in a bitter way. "Oh yeah, I guess she did that. But not exactly in the right order."

"She thought getting married was going to make things better," I said. "And I think you agreed with her."

"Well, I guess we were both wrong. Look at how that turned out." She shook her head. "What a mess. But it's probably what she deserves—she needed to deal with the consequences of her sin."

"Well, then it probably won't make you feel better to learn that they're getting an annulment."

She looked skeptical. "An annulment?"

So without going into too much detail, I explained the rationale.

"That's convenient."

"Aren't you happy for Nat?"

She shrugged. "What about the baby? How is Natalie going to raise a child on her own? Being a single mom is no picnic, you know. And if she thinks she can drag that child back here and expect me to support them, she'd better think again."

"The baby has been adopted."

"Adopted?" Mrs. McCabe looked truly shocked now. "Adopted by whom? When did this happen?"

"On the day she was born."

"She?" Mrs. McCabe's features softened a little. "The baby was a girl?"

"You didn't know?"

"Your dad forgot to mention it."

"And you didn't even ask?"

"It was early in the morning, Kim. Christmas Day. I wasn't thinking terribly clearly."

"And then you didn't even come to see her—to see them."

She just shook her head.

"The baby was eight pounds, five ounces. A very beautiful baby girl. Blond hair, blue eyes. They thought she looked like Natalie." Okay, I wasn't sure if I was saying this for her benefit or to hurt her. But I figured she might as well hear the details.

"They?"

"The adoptive parents."

"Oh..." She seemed to be processing this, and I'm not sure if she was happy with the news or not.

"They seemed very nice."

"Is it an open adoption?"

"No."

"But Natalie met the parents?"

"Just briefly and only by first names. It's how Nat wanted it. She wanted to be assured that they were good people. But they live in another state and won't have any contact with each other—unless after the baby grows up, she wants to meet her birth mother. It's all written up in a legal contract."

"When—I mean how—did all this happen?"

So I explained to her about the adoption agency. How my dad encouraged Natalie to look into it and how she finally came to this decision.

"So what now?" Mrs. McCabe looked to be at a loss just then. As if hearing that her daughter's messy life had been all cleaned up without a bit of help from her was slightly disturbing. Or maybe she was feeling guilty. I hoped it was the latter.

"What do you mean?" I asked. "What now?"

"What's Natalie going to do now?"

"Do now?" I thought about this. "Well, I guess she's going to recover from the birth experience—which was not easy, by the way."

"I didn't expect that it would be."

"And she and Ben will get their annulment. And maybe she'll want to go back to Harrison now and graduate with her class."

"You think they'll allow that?"

"I don't know why not."

"Seems to me she'd be too embarrassed to show her face there...especially considering all she's been through."

"I think she can deal with it," I said with a slight edge to my voice, "especially considering all she's been through."

"I know you think I'm a terrible mother, Kim."

Now this made me feel slightly rotten, like why was I being so hard on her, and what about my prayer to say the right things? "No, I don't think you're a terrible mother,

Mrs. McCabe. And I know you've been through some rough times, and it's not easy raising kids on your own."

"That's true enough. Then having a pregnant teenager on top of everything else. Sometimes I wonder how much more I can take."

"You're not the only one who's been hurt by all this. I mean, I don't think anyone was too happy when Natalie got pregnant. Other than her worst enemies, anyway. And I'll admit that I was really mad at her for a while too. I felt like she was ruining my life as well as hers. But I had to forgive her and get on with it. And once I did that, I started to realize how Natalie was the one who was suffering the most. I mean, if you think she needed to 'deal with the consequences of her sin,' as you put it, you should be really, really happy. Because she's been beat up—a lot. And she's still hurting now. She thinks you hate her."

"I don't hate her..."

I just stared at Mrs. McCabe then. I wanted to accuse her of lying, but I controlled myself.

"I hate the sin," she continued, "not the sinner."

"That might sound good to you, but, you know, we're all sinners. Don't you remember when the crowds brought that woman to Jesus, and they wanted to stone her? Don't you remember what Jesus told them?"

She kind of blinked then.

"What's so different about Natalie's situation? Well, except for the fact that she wasn't an adulteress and she hadn't slept with a bunch of men?"

Mrs. McCabe nodded.

"Why can't you forgive her?" I finally said, my last desperate attempt to bring some resolution for my best friend.

But she didn't answer me. So I stood up, excused myself, and left.

But later today, Mrs. McCabe came over. And she and Natalie went into the guest room where Nat's been staying and had a long talk. They were in there for a couple of hours. And finally—finally—they came out and announced that all was forgiven and that both of them were sorry and that they'd hugged and made up and everything was just fine. Just like that.

"I guess I'm going home now," Nat told me with a smile. And she and her mom packed up her stuff, and with my help we moved her back home.

And now it looks like it's just me and my dad again. And I get to go back to living my own life. And that's totally cool with me!

Dear Jamie,

I'm making my New Year's resolutions now. Actually, I'm just making one. But I'm worried because it seems like every time I make New Year's resolutions, I just end up blowing them the following week. Anyway, I thought if I secretly told someone (like you), I might make it work this year. My resolution is to quit smoking. My parents both smoke, and it doesn't bother them that I smoke. Except when I sneak their cigarettes. Then they get mad. I've smoked for two years now, and I'll be seventeen pretty soon. I really want to kick this disgusting habit, and I think I can do it. Any suggestions?

Sick of Smoking

Dear SOS,

Congratulations! They say half the battle of breaking a habit is deciding to do it. But I've also heard that smoking is VERY addictive. So you might need help. Have you considered using gum or a patch? Or are you sure you can really pull this off cold turkey? Anyway, here are some tips I found online. I hope they're helpful. Good luck!

- *Set a quit date and stick to it.*
- *Avoid being around smokers.*
- *Make a list of your reasons for quitting.*
- *Tell everyone you're quitting. Don't be secretive.*
- *Talk to your doctor for additional help.*
- *Replace smoking with other activities, like taking a walk, calling a friend, or starting a new hobby.*
- *Reduce stress in your life by doing things you enjoy.*
- *Reward yourself every day for not smoking.*
- *Drink plenty of water and other fluids.*
- *Take it one day at a time.*

Just Jamie

Fourteen

Monday, January 8

If I was happy to go back to school last fall, I think I was even happier today. And that's because Nat came back to school with me. Okay, it was a little awkward at first. She got the standard stares, whispers, glances, catty comments, snide smirks... But I was so impressed with how she handled it. We'd done some "rehearsing" of funny comebacks to prepare for those inevitable moments when someone stupid might say or do something totally moronic. And Nat pulled it off brilliantly. Humor can really take the edge off.

At lunchtime we sat with Cesar, Jake, and Allie, and just as we expected, Marissa and Spencer showed up and took their jabs at Nat.

"Something is different..." Marissa said to Nat with this evil twinkle in her eye. "Oh yeah, you're not pregnant anymore." Then she frowned, eying Nat's baggy shirt, which is helping to conceal her still-rather-bulky waistline. "Or are you?"

"Actually, I was pregnant with twins," Nat told her with a straight face. "One was born during Christmas break, and I'm waiting to have the other one during spring break."

Fortunately this made the guys laugh. And I think it actually made Marissa see Nat in a different light.

"So are you and Ben still married or not?" Spencer asked Nat.

"Turns out we never were," Nat tossed back at him. "I think it was just a figment of everyone's imagination."

"So where's Ben now?" he persisted.

"Ben's going to graduate from McFadden," Cesar informed him.

"Big chicken." Spencer made a face.

"Actually..." Nat turned serious. "He's been pretty brave if you think about it. I mean, how many of you would've been willing to go through what he went through?"

"Get married and have kids while you're in high school?" Spencer rolled his eyes. "You can call it brave if you want. I call it plain stupid."

"Yeah," Nat agreed. "I can't really argue with you on that."

"Even so," said Allie, "it's good to know that God is bigger than our biggest mistakes. He can fix anything—if we let Him."

And then, just like that, the subject changed, and when no one was looking I winked at Nat. She smiled back. And I'm thinking life is going to get back to normal soon. Well, whatever "normal" is. Maybe it doesn't exist.

Not to suggest that Nat hasn't been affected by all this. She definitely has. And sometimes I see this really sad expression in her eyes, and I know she's hurting inside. Probably in ways I'll never understand. And yet she seems to have changed in some really positive ways as well. She's way more humble and compassionate. She even treats Marissa differently—and she used to hate that girl. And I don't think she's going to be preaching at any of us anytime soon. Not that she's turned her back on God. If anything, I think it's the opposite. It's like she's gotten deeper in a spiritual sense.

I think Nat's relationship with God went to a level that she'd never before experienced. Not that I'd recommend going through what she went through to reach this place. But I have to agree with Allie—God really can bring good out of bad if you let Him. But He definitely won't force it on you.

Friday, January 19

I got to jam with Redemption at the Paradiso tonight. It was so cool. We played some pretty mellow stuff—a real change from the rockier kinds of things they usually play at concerts. But I thought it sounded awesome. And, okay, I suppose I entertained this teeny, tiny fantasy that maybe they'd invite me to join them on tour. Of course, I'd have to really think twice about that since I'm pretty committed to finishing high school here and they'll be leaving to tour again in March. Allie will do her schoolwork on the road and then come back to walk with our class at graduation. So even if they did ask (which I'm sure they won't), I'd probably have to decline. Oh, well.

Thursday, January 25

Something very weird happened today. As usual, I picked up our mail when I got home, and there was one of those cards that tells you there's something you need to pick up at the post office. Thinking it could be something important for Dad, I decided to stop by there on my way to work at the Paradiso. But it turned out to be a registered letter for me—in a large cardboard envelope that was sent from South Korea. I was running a little late, so I just stuck the envelope in my bag and drove as fast I dared, since it was icy out, over to the Paradiso so I could relieve Chloe from her shift.

"Sorry I'm late," I tell her. "I stopped at the post office."

"No problem." She's already grabbing her jacket. "It's been really quiet in here today. But that's probably because of the cruddy weather. I gotta get going. We're supposed to be at the church to meet Willy for practice in like three minutes—and our manager can get a little testy if we're late. Cesar is supposed to be here by five."

"Be careful," I say. "It's icy out there."

"The forecast is saying snow by nightfall," she calls as she goes out the front door, the little bell tinkling behind her.

I glance out at the murky gray sky and figure the weather forecast is probably going to be right this time. Then I look around the cozy café to see if any tables need to be wiped down or bins refilled or whatever. But everything seems to be in tip-top shape. Even the condiment jars look recently filled. And all the machines are shining. It must've been really slow in here today.

I decide to take advantage of this lull by retrieving my mysterious letter from my bag. Inside the heavy envelope is a single sheet of very lightweight paper. I think I've heard it called onion skin, but I didn't know that people actually still used it. The words on this page are typewritten, but not like a computer. More like an old-fashioned typewriter, like the one my dad keeps in his office "for old time's sake." With hands that are shaking ever so slightly, I begin to read. I have a feeling I know what this is about.

5 January

Dear Miss Kim Peterson:

I write to introduce myself to you. My name is Lee Jin-Soon. I was born in Po'hang, South Korea, in August 1964. I graduated from Puson National University in 1986. I work for a large international corporation located in Puson. I am not married. I am a modern woman of independence. I enjoy travel and music and theatre and art. I have been on all continents except North America.

I do not know how to say this, except to simply write it on paper. I am your birth mother. For many years I have pretended that your birth did not occur. But now you are becoming a young woman, and I know you must have questions. I recently contacted the orphanage where I left you almost eighteen years ago. Miss Young told me that you had made inquiries of me. I am happy to make your acquaintance, if that would be pleasing to you.

Sincerely,

Lee Jin-Soon

enclosures: photograph, business card

Now my hands are really shaking. This letter is actually from my birth mother! The woman who brought me into this world. Her name is Lee Jin-Soon. I reread the letter again, more carefully now, taking in each fact and thoroughly processing it. She's in her forties. She sounds like a normal, intelligent person, a career woman who lives in a large city. (I know from previous research that Puson is the second largest city in South Korea; Seoul is the largest.) She seems to live comfortably and travels quite a bit. Not a bad life.

Okay, this is nothing like the pitiful woman I've often imagined—the young, impoverished, desperate prostitute who was forced to give up her baby to survive on the streets. As I finish the letter the second time through, I notice the note at the bottom says "enclosures: photograph, business card." I grab the envelope and look inside, and sure enough, wedged into a corner is a small black-and-white photograph of a pretty Korean woman. I study her features, trying to decide if she looks like me or not. But other than the classic Asian features, I'm not so sure.

I look in the envelope again and notice a small white business card also wedged in the corner. The name of the company isn't familiar, but beneath Lee Jin-Soon's name is what I assume must be her title: Director of Foreign Services. I'm not sure what that means, but it does sound impressive.

And yet I am not impressed. If anything, I am irritated. I put the letter and other pieces back in the envelope, and just as I slip them into my bag, I'm relieved to see a couple who appear to be coming into the coffeehouse.

I distract myself with waiting on these kids, faces that are vaguely familiar; although, I'm pretty sure they attend McFadden. But I treat them like old friends as I take their orders, and we talk about how cold it is outside, and they tell me about the wreck they saw on Forty-Ninth and Berger on their way over here.

"There were two ambulances," the short blond girl tells me.

"I hope it's not too serious," I say as I hand her a cappuccino.

"Well, it was serious for the car," the guy says. "It was totaled."

Business in the coffeehouse picks up just a little. Not enough to be overwhelming, but I appreciate the distraction from my somewhat disturbing letter. I consider calling my dad, although he'd still be at work, or even Natalie. But I'm not really sure what I'd say. I just feel this need to tell someone about it.

Finally, just a little before five, the coffeehouse is completely empty and I'm thinking this could be a good night to close early, but then Cesar comes in and looks like he's ready to go to work.

"It's pretty dead in here," I tell him as I start to take off my apron.

He nods. "I see that. But maybe it'll pick up later this evening."

"I don't know," I tell him. "The weather might be keeping people inside."

"Well, if it's too slow, I might call Chloe and see what she says."

I pick up my bag, but as I swing it up, it turns upside down—emptying most of the contents all over the black and white checkerboard floor. I make a groaning sound and stoop to pick my junk up, shoving it back into my bag.

Cesar bends down to help, finally handing me the large envelope. "That looks interesting."

I stand up, still holding the envelope and frowning at it, as if it has personally offended me.

"Bad news?"

"Not exactly." I start to shove it into my bag then stop. "Just something really weird."

"Weird?" He kind of smiles. "That sounds intriguing."

"You want to hear about it?"

"Pull up a stool," he tells me. "I'll pour you a drink."

I laugh. "You sound like a bartender."

"I am. Just happens to be a coffee bar. You want the regular?"

I nod. And as he's fixing my mocha, I pull out the letter and the photograph. When Cesar sets my mocha in front of me, I hold up the photo. "Do you think this looks like me?"

He studies the photo, then looks at me. "Maybe..." He studies it again. "But you're prettier."

I kind of blink at that. "Really? You think so?"

He laughs. "Yeah. But who is that?"

"My birth mother."

He slowly nods. "Ahh."

"It's the first time she's ever contacted me, and I think I'm kind of in shock."

"I can understand that."

So then I pour out the story about how I've always

assumed the worst when it came to my birth mom. "Well, except for the times when I imagined that she was royalty and that I was actually a princess who'd been stolen at birth. But I eventually outgrew those fantasies and just settled on the most realistic explanation."

"So, aren't you pleased to discover that she's a well-educated, intelligent woman who's living a fulfilling life?"

I frown at the photo still in my hand. "You'd think that I'd be happy to find that out..."

"But you're not?"

"It just raises a whole bunch of new questions."

"Like?"

"Like why did she give me up?"

"Maybe you should ask her."

"Maybe."

"But you're not sure."

"The truth is, I'm not sure I want to have anything to do with her."

"Why not?"

"I don't know..." I look out the window and notice that a few snowflakes are starting to fall. "Maybe it's because of my mom—my real mom."

He nods, as if he gets this. "Like it would be disloyal to your real mom to get to know your birth mother?"

"Maybe." I take a slow sip of my coffee.

"I wonder what your real mom would say about that."

I sigh. "Yeah, that's probably a good point. I'm sure

she'd encourage me to get to know this woman. I'm just not sure if I'm ready for that yet."

"Sounds like the ball is in your court, Kim. It's not like she can force herself on you—living halfway around the world, that is."

"That is a comfort."

"Maybe you just need some time to let this news settle," he says as he wipes a small spill of coffee from the counter. "Take it to God and see what He's telling you to do."

"You're right." I'm looking at the photo again. And even though this woman is in her forties, she's still very good-looking. "You really think I'm prettier than her?" I ask Cesar, instantly wishing I hadn't.

He laughs. "Oh, you know that I think you're pretty, Kim. I've told you before that if I was into dating, you'd definitely be on my A-list."

I shake my head. "Too bad."

He nods. "Yep. Too bad."

"Would Chloe still be on that list?" Don't ask me why I say this. Maybe I'm just stalling before I have to leave this warm place and face the elements on my way home.

"Chloe's heart belongs to Jeremy Baxter," Cesar says. This is old news, of course, but not anything that I've heard Cesar talk much about.

"And you're okay with that?"

"Of course. Chloe and I have only been friends for several years now. I wouldn't have it any other way."

So then I ask Cesar about where he's going to school next year, and he mentions several possibilities, including Bible college. "I think God might be calling me into some kind of ministry," he says quietly.

"Really?"

"I haven't actually told anyone, besides Josh. Because I'm not sure. Maybe I'm just hoping. Anyway, I'd appreciate it if you kept that under your hat."

"No problem." I slip the letter and things back in the envelope. "Maybe the same with me. Not that anyone would really care about my birth mom. But I think I'd like to keep it quiet for a while. Until I can figure out what I'm going to do."

Cesar grins. "And like any other trustworthy bartender playing therapist, your secrets are safe with me."

I finish my coffee and notice that it's five-thirty. "Well, my dad will be getting home soon. Guess I better go."

"Be safe out there," he says as I pull on my coat.

"You too."

"Yeah. I might even close early if it's too comatose."

But when I get home there's a message from Dad on our machine saying that he has to work late and to go ahead and eat dinner without him. I leave him a plate in the fridge, then come to my room to write in my diary, do my homework, and think about this new development with my birth mother.

And as much as I hate to admit this, I'm really resenting her intrusion into my life. Every time I look at her photo, I imagine this very smug, self-centered woman who only thinks about herself. And then I wonder if she could be lying about the whole thing. Maybe she's really just dirt-poor and pathetic but doesn't want me to know. She could've had someone else write this letter. But how do you explain the business card? Of course, I'm sure anyone can get anything printed if they want.

Maybe she has ulterior motives. Maybe she thinks we're rich and she can hit us up for money. Or maybe she's not my birth mother at all. Oh, I know I'm being ridiculous. But it does make me wonder.

Dear Jamie,

I just made a new friend, and she is so cool. We have such a great time together, and I think we could maybe even become best friends. The problem is that her family is pretty well-off. I mean, they are rich. But my parents are divorced, and I live with my mom, and we are not rich—not even close. But I've been hiding this from my friend. In fact, I've acted like we're rich too. I even came up with an explanation for my clothes, which are not designer labels, saying that my mom and I refuse to support the corrupt fashion industry by wasting money on expensive clothes—like this is our personal political protest. And I think my friend believes me. But I know I can't keep this charade up. What should I do?

Fake Friend

Dear FF,

I think you already know what to do. Tell your friend the truth. The sooner the better. And if she's as cool as you think, I'm guessing she'll forgive you for lying and not hold any lack of material wealth against you. You sound like a smart person who's fun to hang with. Hopefully she already recognizes this, and you guys will be friends for a long time to come.

Just Jamie

Fifteen

Monday, January 29

I still haven't responded to the letter from my supposed birth mother. But I did tell my dad and Nat about it, and although they both encouraged me to correspond with her, they also agreed that it was my decision to make and that I should ultimately do whatever I'm comfortable with.

"It's possible that your gut instincts are telling you something," my dad finally said. "You need to listen to your heart, Kim. There might be a reason you feel the way you do."

"Like this woman might be a fraud?"

"It wouldn't be hard to find out," he told me. "I could even put one of my researchers on her. Make sure she's the real thing before you get involved."

"Would you do that, Dad?"

"Of course. I'd be glad to. There are a lot of exploiters out there. I certainly don't want you getting involved with one."

So I figure this buys me some time for now. When Dad gets back to me with the facts, I can decide what to do.

"Aren't you curious?" Nat asked me on our way home from school today. "I mean, wouldn't you love to talk to her, to see what she's like, and to ask her questions about why she gave you up?"

"I don't know..."

"You used to be obsessed with finding your birth mom," she reminds me. "Remember how you did that exhaustive Internet search? You were relentless, Kim."

"That was then..." I told her. "Back when I was trying to figure out who I was and why I was here and all those questions that hammered away at me in my early teens. I think I've grown up a lot since then."

"So you really know who you are now?" Her voice had a teasing edge to it.

"Well, not completely, but it is getting better. Finding God made a pretty huge difference too."

"So you'd really be okay never knowing the woman who gave birth to you, the one who's genetically responsible for who you are?"

"I think God's the one who's genetically responsible for who I am, Nat."

"I know, I know. But I guess I like to think about the part of me that's in my baby...even if I never get to see her again. I mean, it's so amazing to think that there's a little girl out there who—" Then Nat's voice broke, and I could see tears in her eyes.

"I'm sorry. Maybe we shouldn't be talking about this."

"It's okay, Kim. It's not your fault. Steph keeps telling me that it's going to take time, maybe the rest of my life, to get over this."

"How's the counseling going?" I asked, ready to change the subject to something more comfortable for both of us.

"Steph is great. She's really helping me to work through this. Hey, maybe you should go talk to her about this thing with your birth mom. I'll bet she'd have some ideas."

"I'm going to wait until Dad finds out whether or not she's legit."

"Yeah, that's probably smart. But I think she's the real deal, Kim. That letter sounded sincere to me."

I didn't point out to her that it could've been created to sound sincere, that con artists are usually good at tricking people. I think it's better to just wait and see. In the meantime, I'm not really thinking about it much.

Thursday, February 8

"Good news," my dad announced when he got home from work tonight. "My researcher informed me that his resources confirmed that Lee Jin-Soon is who she says she is. And he's even discovered birth records that match Lee Jin-Soon's claim to be your mother. Other than a DNA test, which is the only way to be 100 percent sure, this woman appears to be telling the truth."

"Oh."

"Aren't you glad to hear this?"

"I guess." I looked down at my hands.

"You know, it doesn't change anything, Kim. It's your choice whether or not you respond to the letter. I think the only reason she took the liberty to write you is because the Korean orphanage knew that you'd tried to locate your birth mother several years ago. Otherwise, you probably never would've heard from her at all. Don't you think?"

"I suppose. But I was only fifteen when I was trying to find her. I didn't know what I was doing."

Dad laughed. "You've always known what you were doing, Kim. You were just born that way."

I had to smile at that. "Maybe, but I'm not sure I really want to write back. Not yet anyway."

"Does this have to do with your mom?"

"Partly. But it's more than that. I mean, I know Mom would want me to get to know this woman. But I also know she wouldn't push me."

"I'm not pushing you, honey. At least I hope not."

"You're not, Dad."

"You're a smart girl, Kim. I know you'll figure out the right thing to do. I have complete faith in you." Then he handed me a large manila envelope. "Here's the research. You might want to just file it for a later date."

And so that's what I did. But something about Dad's statement—about having complete faith in me—reminds me that I haven't totally put this thing with my birth mother into God's hands. And I think it's time that I do. First I spend some time reading my Bible, and then I actually get down on my knees. And believe me, I don't always do this, but it amazes me how awesome it can be. I pray that God will take the whole birth mother dilemma and show me what to do. Finally I say, "God, if you want Lee Jin-Soon to be part of my life, then I am willing. Just help me to know Your will, and help me to do it. Amen."

Saturday, February 10

I wrote to my birth mother yesterday. It wasn't a terribly personal letter. In fact, it reminded me a lot of the one she wrote me. So maybe we are related, after all. It was a one-pager with very brief descriptions of who I am and what I like to do. Almost like a résumé. But, hey, it was better than nothing. Also, I included a photo. I just picked up my senior photos, which aren't bad.

I mailed the letter today. Maybe this will be the end of it. We've exchanged photos and some bare-bones information. Maybe that's enough. The only reason I wrote the letter yesterday was because I'd gotten this very definite impression that God wanted me to do this. And in the last paragraph of my letter, I told my birth mother about how I had looked into Buddhism and how it didn't work for me. Then I told her about how I found God and how my life has been changed ever since. I also told her that God loved her and wanted to have a relationship with her as well. So, if nothing else, this woman has at least heard a bit of the gospel. Even if it is just a sliver. Who knows?

Wednesday, February 14

We had a Valentine's party at the Paradiso last night. It was Cesar's idea originally, but a bunch of kids from youth group helped out. We called our little gathering The Lonely Hearts Club, but that was only because we were doing it for kids who weren't going to the Valentine's Dance.

And as it turned out, it wasn't such a little gathering. The coffeehouse was pretty jam-packed. But it was fun. In fact, I think it was probably better than the dance. The theme was the seventies, and everyone who dressed up received a free chocolate heart. Chloe hired a DJ, and some of us even danced. It was really an awesome evening. While in the restroom, we actually heard one girl say how she was surprised that a party without booze could be this fun.

"And with no hangover," I pointed out.

"And no arrests," added Allie.

Go figure.

Wednesday, February 21

I received another letter from my birth mother today. This one was sent through regular airmail and was very short and somewhat shocking. I'm not even sure what to think. Or how to respond.

13 February

Dear Miss Kim,

Thank you for your letter of 7 February. It was a great pleasure to hear from you. I plan to travel to the United States the following month for business and pleasure. I would like to meet you and your family if this is convenient to your schedule.

If possible, I would like to communicate with you through electronic mail. Do you use the Internet? If so, please respond to me at the following address.

leejinsoon@ixpcn.com

Sincerely,

Lee Jin-Soon

Okay, now what? It's one thing to agree to write to her—like maybe one or two letters. But do I really want to meet this woman in person? I'm not so sure. But instead of freaking, I go straight to God. I put it in His hands and ask Him to lead me. And when I say amen, I know that it's going to be okay. Well, mostly. I guess I still feel a little nervous.

When Dad gets home, I tell him the news. And he seems just fine.

"That's great, Kim. I would love to meet her."

"You would?"

"Of course. She's your birth mother. You're my daughter. Why wouldn't I want to meet her?"

I nod. "Okay..."

"But it's up to you. It's your call, sweetheart. If you're not comfortable with this, you just explain to her that it's not a good time."

"I don't even know when exactly," I admit. "She only said March."

"Well, why don't you e-mail her for clarification? If it makes you feel better, don't commit to anything yet. Just let her know that you're considering it."

"That's a good idea."

But it's getting pretty late when I finally get around to e-mailing her. First I do my homework and practice my violin, and then I play about seven games of spider solitaire, all of which I ace. Finally I figure I might as well get this over with. So I go online and find a world time chart, which indicates that Korea is about twelve hours ahead of us, which according to my calculations means that it's mid-morning there by the time I start writing my message.

Dear Lee Jin-Soon,

I'm responding to your letter. As you can see, I do use e-mail. And I prefer it to regular mail, which we sometimes call "snail mail" since it's so slow. What dates are you thinking about for your visit in March? It's possible that we won't be home.

Sincerely,

Kim Peterson

Okay, I know that's not totally true. But on the other hand, it's not a lie either. It's entirely possible that Dad and I will go somewhere during spring break. Who knows? To my surprise, I'm still online when I see that I've got a new mail. And, of course, it is from Lee Jin-Soon.

Dear Miss Kim,

Thank you for your e-mail. My travel dates in March are flexible. What dates will you be available to meet with me? I will adjust my travel to fit your schedule. Thank you.

Sincerely,

Lee Jin-Soon

Dear Lee Jin-Soon,

My spring break at school goes from March 22 to March 30. It's possible that we might be gone

during this week. Other than that, I think we will be home.
Sincerely,
Kim Peterson

As soon as I hit send, I know that there's no way to get out of this. But even so, I pray that God won't let her come unless there's some really good reason for her to be here. And I'm hoping that's not going to be the case. I wait at my computer, expecting her to respond immediately, just like last time. But after about twenty minutes and winning four more games of solitaire, I decide that she's probably not going to respond. Well, good! I'm about to sign off and shut down my computer when I see the little flag indicating that new mail has arrived.

Dear Miss Kim,
I have checked my calendar, and I would like to come see you during the second week of March. I will arrive on 10 March. I will make my own accommodation arrangements. If it is possible, I would like to take your family to dinner on 11 March. Is this acceptable to you?
Sincerely,
Lee Jin-Soon

Well, I have to admit that she doesn't seem to be asking too much of us. But then I wonder if this could possibly be some kind of set-up. Could she be pretending that she'll only be here briefly, and then decide to move in for good and empty my dad's bank account? Okay, that's pretty paranoid. Besides, Dad said his researcher confirmed that she's really who she claims to be. Maybe I should just agree and get this thing over with. But before I e-mail back, I check with my dad first. Just to make sure he doesn't have other plans. Unfortunately, he is free March 11. It seems I have no more excuses.

Dear Lee Jin-Soon,
The dates you mentioned appear to work for us. We look forward to seeing you on March 11. I have a question. I've noticed that you refer to me as "Miss Kim" in your letters. Should I call you Miss Jin-Soon? Or Miss Soon? Or Miss Lee Jin-Soon? I don't know what's proper in Korean. By the way, you may just call me Kim.
Sincerely,
Kim

Dear Kim,
It seems odd to call you "Kim" without Miss in front of it. But I will try. I am guessing that your first name is not Peterson because that sounds like a man's name. And I remember now how Americans put their family names after. So is your personal name Kim? My family name is Lee. But my personal name is Jin-Soon, and my

close friends call me Jin. I would like you to call me Jin too, if you are comfortable with this. I must admit that this is all very strange and awkward for me. I am not used to thinking that I am a mother of a nearly grown young woman. So far, I have told no friends about my American daughter.

Sincerely,

Jin

For the first time, this woman is beginning to sound more like a real person to me. I feel relieved that she's not comfortable with this new relationship either. It actually gives me hope. And so I write her once more.

Dear Jin,

This is strange for me too. Although my friends know that I'm adopted, I have only told a couple of friends about you. I do want to meet you, but I should probably tell you that my mother (the woman who raised me) died last year. And I think that although she would want me to meet you, it is bothering me a little. Because I know that no one will ever replace my mother. Her name was Patricia, and she was the kindest woman I've ever known.

Sincerely,

Kim

I'm almost ready to go to bed now. I'm concerned that I may have offended Jin with my last e-mail. I guess I just wanted to be honest. Hopefully she won't misread it and think that I'm blowing her off.

Dear Kim,
I am so sorry that your mother has passed on. She sounds like she was a wonderful woman. I am so very thankful to hear that you have been in a good home. I did worry about you, but I also kept myself very busy with my studies and my work. I do not think I mentioned in my previous correspondence that you are a very beautiful girl. I am looking at your photograph with amazement. You look very much like my mother's picture when she was young. I will bring some family photographs and other things with me when I come to see you. You may be interested to know what your birth roots look like. I so look forward to meeting you in person.
Sincerely,
Jin

Maybe it's the comment about my photograph reminding me of her mother, but even though I am determined to go to bed since it's nearly midnight now, I decide to write one last note.

Dear Jin,
It's very late here. Almost midnight. But thank you for your kind words. I would love to see photos of your relatives. And I look forward to seeing you in person too.
Good night,
Kim

Sixteen

Sunday, February 25

I am eighteen today! To celebrate, Dad took Nat and me to a new French restaurant that opened last month. Really swanky. Nat and I both got dressed up, and Dad even put on a tie and sports coat for the occasion.

"We make a pretty impressive trio," I told him as he escorted us into the restaurant, a girl on each arm.

He glanced around, looking slightly uncomfortable. "Goodness, I hope people don't think you beautiful girls are actually my dates."

"Why not?" I teased.

"Because all the men will be pea green with envy, and the women will think that I'm robbing the cradle."

Nat and I laughed at his joke, and soon we were seated at a very choice table. Then in honor of my birthday, my dad ordered a bottle of sparkling cider.

"With champagne glasses," he instructed the waiter. "Since we're celebrating my daughter's eighteenth birthday."

The waiter seemed to get into the festivities and treated me like I was a celebrity. So much so that another party at a nearby table kept looking at us like they were trying to figure out who we were. Pretty cool. Not to mention that the food was awesome.

"Do you think we should bring Jin here when she comes?" I asked Dad as we were having dessert—some amazing chocolate confection with a name I can't even begin to pronounce, let alone spell. Maybe I should've taken French instead of Spanish.

"I wonder what she'd think of it," he said. "Being Korean and all. It might not appeal to her."

"She sounds pretty well traveled to me. I'm guessing she's had French food before."

"Then, by all means," he said. "Let's bring her here."

Nat frowned. "I hope I get to meet her. Is she really only going to be here a couple of days?"

"Sounds like it," I told her. "But I'll try to make sure you at least get to meet her once. Maybe if we like her, we'll invite her over to the house."

Dad laughed. "And if we don't like her?"

"We'll tell her that we moved."

Of course, I'm sure that won't be the case. In fact, in just the past couple of weeks of correspondence, I've started to think that I actually do like her. Okay, I don't really know her that well, and her writing tends to be a bit formal at times, but then she'll show a glimpse of who she really is, or how she feels about something, and then she comes across as fairly human and actually pretty nice.

I still have a lot of questions. And I'm actually starting to compile a list, although the list keeps changing. But I figure by the time Jin gets here, I'll have it mostly figured out. I mean, I don't want to assault her with everything at once. And I realize I can still ask her questions through e-mail later on. But at least I'll have something to say if the conversation stalls at all.

She sent me a birthday card and a gift that came just a couple of days before my birthday. I could tell by the box that it was jewelry, but I was surprised at the quality of the necklace, a very large oval-shaped pearl, set in what looked like really nice gold. I showed it to Dad, and he let out a low whistle. "That must've been expensive."

"I hope it didn't set her back too much," I told him. "I mean, I get the feeling she's comfortable and everything, but she does work pretty hard too."

"I wouldn't worry about it. She gave this to you because she wanted to, Kim. Even if it did set her back...well, you just never know, it might be a good thing for her."

So I'm not going to worry about it. But I did send her a thank-you through e-mail. I figured she'd want to know that I'd received it. And then I wore it for my birthday dinner tonight, and I must say I felt like a million bucks. Although I did worry that I might lose it. That would be sad.

Saturday, March 10

I know that Jin was supposed to arrive in town today. But she explained that her flight would get in fairly late and that she'd just settle into her downtown hotel and then meet us for dinner the following evening. And here's what's funny—I was the one who was all worried about her coming, and whether or not I even wanted to see her—and now I'm feeling all impatient, like I can't believe she's in the same town and I don't even get to see her until tomorrow night. I'm halfway tempted to go over to her hotel tomorrow, but I won't do that. I will respect her privacy and wait. Even if the anticipation is killing me!

Sunday, March 11

"You'd think this was a big date or something," I say to Nat, who has come over to lend me her moral support as well as fashion expertise.

I change my outfit about six times before we finally decide on a simple black skirt and a pale gray turtleneck sweater.

"It's simple but sophisticated," Nat assures me.

"Not boring but blah?" I ask as she latches my pearl necklace around my neck.

"Cashmere is not boring, Kim." She runs her hand down the sleeve. "Your dad sure has good taste for an old dude."

I laugh as I check out my image in the mirror again. "And this necklace actually looks pretty good against the gray."

"I wish I could be a mouse in your pocket," Natalie says as I tug on a tall black boot. Nat insisted that this was a boot outfit.

"I don't have any pockets," I point out.

"You know what I mean."

"I promise to tell you everything," I say as I pull on the other boot. "How's that?"

"Very glamorous." She nods with approval.

I check myself out one more time and decide she's right. "Sometimes simple really is better."

"Told you so."

"Here." She hands me my trench coat. "It's coming down in buckets out there. And you might want an umbrella too."

"Dad always has one in his car."

Then Nat hugs me. "Well, have a good time, okay? And call me as soon as you get home."

I nod. "And if I really like Jin, I'll invite her to come to the house tomorrow. If she's not already going home, that is."

Nat crosses her fingers. "Let's hope not."

"And Dad's taking the camera. At the very least we'll have some pics to show you."

I'm a bundle of nerves as Dad drives us downtown. It does feel like a date. Like what if she doesn't like me? What if I don't like her? What if we can't think of anything to say? What if I spill soup in my lap or talk all night with spinach in my teeth?

"Just relax," Dad says as I fidget with the belt of my coat. "This is going to be fun, Kim. Just take it easy and remember to breathe."

"Breathe..." I say, taking in a slow deep breath. "Yes, that's good."

He laughs. "If it makes you feel any better, I'll bet that Jin is even more nervous than you right now."

"Why aren't you nervous?"

He shrugs. "Me? Why, I'm just an old newspaperman, Kim. It takes a lot to get me nervous."

Because it's still pouring outside, my dad actually splurges for valet parking, and we dash in under the awning to avoid getting drenched. A man takes our dripping coats, and Dad gives our names to the hostess. We wait for a minute or so, until we're led to a table that's in a quiet corner on the far side of the restaurant. The table is set for three, but Jin isn't here yet.

"We're a couple minutes early." Dad reaches for the menu. "I'm sure she'll be here soon."

But nearly fifteen minutes pass, and I'm getting worried. "What if I told her the wrong place?" I glance at my watch for like the hundredth time.

"Didn't you give her your cell phone number?"

"What if I gave her the wrong number?"

Dad just laughs now. "Yes, that sounds so much like you, Kim. Getting your numbers all mixed up." Then he nods toward the entrance. "Do you think that's her?"

I see a petite Asian woman talking to the hostess, and now she's being led toward us. I start to stand up, but realize it's too soon, as she's still just walking across the room. She's very stylish—I can see that even from a distance. She walks with confidence and grace. She has on a pale blue suit with a belted jacket and a scarf tucked loosely around her neck. Her shiny black hair is cut in chic layers and goes just below her shoulders, swaying as she walks. As she gets closer, I can see that everything about her is absolute perfection. And I feel like I'm going to faint.

"Breathe," my dad says under his breath.

And then we are standing, introducing ourselves, and I can tell right away that I like her. She seems a little shy and unsure of herself. And yet her eyes sparkle with intelligence, and her English is actually quite good. Almost more natural sounding than the way she writes.

"It is so good to finally meet you, Kim," she tells me as she continues to clasp my hand. "You are even more beautiful than your photograph."

"Thanks. So are you."

She smiles. "For an old woman, you mean?"

"You don't look that old."

She nods. "Oh, you know how we modern women are. We like to stay young for as long as we can."

We all laugh and sit down. Dad asks about her flight

and the hotel, and she says that everything is fine. Then she turns to me. "I just want to keep looking at you. You are really so beautiful, Kim."

Okay, as much as I love compliments, this attention is making me a little uncomfortable. "I'm wearing the necklace you sent." I hold it up as if she can't see.

"It is perfect on you."

"I really love it."

"It was my mother's," she says. "It's not very old. I think it was given to her in the 1930s."

"A family piece?"

She smiles. "Yes..."

Now I'm remembering some of my questions. I do have them with me, neatly printed out and in my purse, but I don't want to look like I'm doing a newspaper interview.

"Are your parents still alive?"

"No. They have both passed."

"Do you have brothers and sisters?"

She nods. "Yes. I have two brothers. One sister. I am the baby."

"Do you see them much?"

She shakes her head sadly. "Oh, no...we are not close. Not anymore."

So I decide not to ask about nieces and nephews. "I studied the South Korean map. It looks like your hometown isn't too far from Puson."

"Yes. That's right."

"So do you have family who still live there? In Po'hang?"

"Yes. They all live there. It is a beautiful place by the Sea of Japan."

Okay, now I'm faced with a tough question. Jin seems to be estranged from her family, and I want to know why. But the waiter is here to tell us about this evening's specials.

"Oh," says Jin, "that sounds lovely." And then she actually translates some of it for us.

"You speak French?" the waiter asks, impressed.

"Oh, just a little."

Since we've already pretty much decided what we want, we place our order and he leaves.

"I'm curious," I begin, deciding to go ahead with my questions. "If your family lives so nearby...why don't you see them?"

She nods again slowly, as if she's considering a response. "Yes, I knew you would want to know about my family, Kim. You see they are a family of influence, a family with considerable wealth. Do you understand?"

I nod, thinking, Hey, she really is royalty.

"And I was the baby of the family." She smiles. "And I was, as I've heard Americans say in the movies, the apple of their eye. I was their precious little pearl. Their darling." She glances at Dad. "I'm sure you must understand."

"Most definitely."

"But my family was very traditional. Very conservative. And I wanted to be a modern woman." Now she holds her chin out firmly. "I did not want to marry the man they had chosen for me. I wanted to go to university, and my teachers were confident that I could easily get my degree. My brothers had gone to university. But not my sister. She was already married with children when I insisted on going to Puson National University. Everyone in our family was shocked when my father agreed. I was the first girl in the family to do this."

"Good for you," my dad says.

"Good and bad." She frowns. "My mother was very angry with me. She told me and the whole family that it would not go well for me, that I would be ruined by this experience. And that if I brought shame to my family, I would not be welcome to come home."

Okay, I have a pretty good idea where this is going.

"This might be hard for you to understand, Kim. You are still young and such a good girl. I could blame it on the influence of American films or my friends, but once I was out of the confining shelter of my home, free to do as I pleased at the university, I made some bad choices. I trusted the wrong people. And during my second year at university, I found myself with child."

We pause as our soup is served. And as usual, my dad bows his head and says a brief prayer.

"I appreciate that you are Christian," Jin says after he's done. "I have read some about Jesus Christ, and I think He was a good man."

I smile at Dad.

"We think so too," he tells her.

"And I don't want to keep asking you uncomfortable questions," I say quickly. "I don't want to spoil this meal with—"

"No, no." She waves her hand. "I want to tell you the truth. Yes, it is humbling to me. But I want you to know everything."

"Okay."

"Yes, okay..." She pauses as if trying to remember where she was in her story. "Oh, yes. I tried to keep my pregnancy secret from my parents. But my mother had spies at the university." She smiles. "Not actual spies, of course. Just friends. Her friends. Not mine. They told her about me."

"She must've been really upset," I say.

"Terribly."

So then I quickly tell her about Natalie and how angry her mother had been, but how she eventually forgave her daughter.

"Not my mother." She firmly shakes her head. "She took her anger to the grave with her."

"That's too bad."

"The only one in my family who will still speak to me is my oldest brother. He is like you—a Christian—and he has forgiven me."

"Good for him."

"Yes. And good for me."

She tells about how she took time off from school,

how the father of the baby gave her money but didn't want to marry her. "I did not want to marry him either," she says. "Except for my shame. But I gave birth at the hospital and when I saw you—" she pauses to look at me again—"I thought you were the most beautiful thing I'd ever seen. And I decided I would keep you.

"But it was not so easy. My parents cut off funds. My boyfriend disappeared. I had a job, but to work and continue my studies and be a mother to an infant…it was just too much. I was overwhelmed, and then I got sick. And finally I remembered the baby home I had seen before. And I asked my friend to take you there for me." She looks down at her untouched soup. "It was a very sad day."

Now Dad reaches over and pats her on the arm. "It was a joyous day for my wife and me. The happiest day of our lives was when we came over to Korea to pick Kim up. You gave us the most precious, wonderful gift, Jin. I can never thank you enough for letting us have her."

Jin nods with tears trickling down her cheeks. She reaches into her purse for a handkerchief and blots her nose. "Yes, yes, I believe you, Mr. Peterson. And I am equally thankful."

Then we all quietly eat our soup for a while. It's good that it's only soup and is easily swallowed. And fortunately it's delicious, a creamy asparagus and chicken soup with a touch of rosemary.

With the hard story out of the way, Jin tells us about

how she got back into college. "My father began to secretly send me money through another friend—a real friend—this time. And although I wasn't welcome in their home, my father saw to it that I completed my education. That meant a lot to me. After that I got a job with a corporation that is owned by a friend of my father's. I never knew if my father helped with this or not. He died shortly after I began to work there. But it is a good place to work, and I have steadily advanced. I have the highest position for a woman."

"Congratulations," I tell her, feeling actually proud.

"Yes. It is a good accomplishment. But not without a price."

"What's that?"

"No marriage, no children, no family."

"Your job doesn't allow you to—"

"No, no...it was my choice at first. With long hours and traveling so much, I knew I wouldn't make a good wife. Certainly not according to the standards I'd grown up with. And then later on, when I was in my thirties and actually considering marriage..." She forces a stiff smile. "I sometimes say that fate dealt me a bad card—but perhaps it was because of my past."

"What happened?" I say this and instantly regret it. "I mean, I totally understand if you don't want to tell us..."

"I became sick." She looks directly at me now, and as if she's not completely comfortable saying this in front of my dad, she lowers her voice. "A female kind of sickness. It resulted in the inability to have children—

ever. And that's when I decided it would be unfair to any husband in my future. And so I have remained single."

Her finely arched brows lift. "Free to do as I please, go where I like. Eat dinner in or out. Date a variety of men or simply stay home and read a book. And truly it's not so bad. Some of my married friends are quite envious." She smiles sadly. "You see, I am a truly modern woman."

By the time we're finished with dinner, I feel like I really know her. "Will you still be in town tomorrow?" I ask as we're leaving the restaurant.

"I can be."

"Would you like to come to our house?" I ask suddenly. "I can fix dinner. I'm not the greatest cook, but I—"

"She's a good cook," my dad assures Jin.

"That sounds lovely."

"My best friend lives down the street, and she really wants to meet you," I explain. "Would you mind if she came too?"

She laughs. "Not at all. I would love to see where you live, Kim. And I would love to meet your friend."

So it's all arranged, and my dad even offers to pick Jin up on his way home from work. And when we get home, I immediately call Nat, fill her in on all the details I can remember, and finally tell her the good news about tomorrow night. And she is ecstatic. "I can't wait to meet her. She sounds so cool."

"Maybe you can come over early and help me?"

"No problem."

"I really want to do this right," I explain. "Jin is kind of sophisticated, and I think she's used to the best, you know. I just really want everything to be as perfect as possible."

Nat laughs. "And to think this was the girl who didn't want to meet her birth mother."

"Yeah, yeah... It's weird, I know."

We chat a little longer then hang up, and I sit down to write all this in my diary. Even as I write, I feel like it's hard to wrap my head around what happened tonight. Just thinking that the classy woman we had dinner with was actually my birth mother, that I have this authentic genetic connection to her. Well, it just seems a little unreal.

Then reality kicks in, and I realize it's Sunday and I need to get some letters for my column done. I wonder if I should tell Jin about this secret part of my life. I mean she is, after all, my birth mother, and she lives so far away. Like who would she tell? I decide to run it by my dad first. But I think it would be cool if I could tell her. I think she'd be impressed. And for some reason I want to impress her. Is that weird?

Dear Jamie,

I totally hate going to school and would do anything to avoid it. I keep asking my mom to let me do homeschool instead, but she says to forget it. The reason I hate school is because of these girls who always pick on me. It's like I'm their favorite form of entertainment—all they do is try to embarrass me and make my life completely miserable. Sometimes I actually want to kill myself. What should I do?

Hopeless

Dear Hopeless,

This is so wrong! And I am so sorry that you have to suffer like this. You need to talk to someone about what's going on. And you need to do it NOW. First you need to tell your parents. And then you need to make an appointment with your school counselor and tell her/him exactly what's going on, hopefully with your parents present. Tell about specific instances, and give names. It's up to the school to make sure that you are safe there. If they can't protect you from bullies, maybe your parents should consider homeschool. I suggest you let them read this letter.

Just Jamie

Seventeen

Monday, March 12

Nat and I went to the grocery store after school today. I had no idea what we were going to fix for dinner, but I wanted it to be something sophisticated.

"No Hamburger Helper tonight," I told Nat as we cruised the aisles with an empty grocery cart.

"Pasta?" she suggested.

"I don't know..."

"Well, you don't want to fix something that's tricky," she warned me. "That could blow up in your face and be really embarrassing."

I was trying to remember what my mom used to do when Dad was having an important business associate over for dinner. I know she did roast sometimes, but I think that took a long time to cook.

"How about fish?" Nat asked as we walked by the seafood section.

"Fish?" I paused with the cart and looked at the various types of fish behind the glass case.

"Can I help you, ladies?" asked a short man with white hair.

"I'm not sure..."

"She's having a special guest for dinner," Nat started to explain. "But she doesn't know what to cook."

He smiled. "We have some nice Atlantic salmon." He pointed to a bright orange piece of fish.

"I've never cooked fish before," I said.

"Oh, it's easy. I even have a recipe right here for baked salmon that almost anyone can make. I have the seasonings all mixed up and everything."

"Really?"

"It only takes about twenty minutes to bake."

The next thing I knew we were getting salmon, and this old guy was recommending what we should have with it. And I have to admit, it did sound easy enough. Small red potatoes that "only take twenty minutes to cook," he told me. "Just put them in when you put the salmon in." Then he recommended a green salad with some special touches and finally told us about a special gourmet bread that would be nice with the salmon. "It's from a new bakery in town."

"What if I mess this up?" I said as we waited in line at the cash register.

"We'll just order in," said Nat.

"Should I get some flowers?" I asked as I noticed some bouquets right by the register.

"Why not?"

So I picked up a pretty arrangement of irises and laid them on top of my other groceries.

"Special night tonight?" the woman at the cash register asked as she started to ring up my purchases.

"It's for her mom," Natalie told the woman.

For some reason that rubbed me wrong, and I tossed Nat a look.

"I mean her birth mom," she added, as if that made it better.

Now I'm sure I was glaring at her.

"Well, that's nice," the woman said as she handed me my change. "I bet my kids will never do anything this nice for me."

"Sorry," Nat told me as soon as we were out of the store. "My mouth just kind of ran away with me."

"It's okay."

"But I don't see why it should bother you, Kim. I mean, she is your birth mom. It's no big deal."

"I know," I told her as I put a bag in my Jeep. And while I did know this, I also knew that something about that conversation bothered me. A lot. And it had to do with my real mom. The one who isn't here anymore. I suddenly felt disloyal to her. And when the cashier mentioned how her kids never did anything like that for her, it got me thinking about how I never did anything like this for my mom. Not really. And that hurt.

"You're being quiet," Nat said as I pulled into my driveway. "I hope I didn't really offend you."

I shook my head and turned off the Jeep. "Just thinking."

We took the stuff inside and started putting it away. But as I moved around in Mom's kitchen, I was feeling worse than ever. I know it sounds crazy, but I felt like I was cheating on my mom. Cheating on her in her own kitchen.

"This is wrong!" I finally said, tossing down the paring knife so it stuck into the cutting board.

"What?" Nat actually jumped.

"Fixing this fancy dinner for Jin. It's so wrong."

Nat frowned. "Why?"

"It's disloyal to my mom." And now I started to cry.

"Oh, Kim." Nat set the lettuce she'd been washing down into the strainer and came over to me and gave me a hug.

"I feel like I'm—like I'm cheating on Mom." I sobbed now. "Like I should've fixed a dinner like this for her when she was here and alive. And instead I'm doing it for Jin—the woman who—who threw me away eighteen years ago!"

Nat patted my back. "She didn't <u>throw</u> you away, Kim. She made a really, really hard choice so that you could have a really, really good life. She made it possible for your mom to have you. Jin gave your mom the most precious gift possible. Your mom never would've had you if it hadn't been for Jin."

I stepped back now, reaching for a paper towel to

wipe my nose. "But why does it feel so wrong then?"

"Because you love your mom. And you miss her. And that's perfectly natural." Nat shrugged.

"But that doesn't really explain it."

"Maybe you feel guilty because you like Jin too. I mean, you didn't want to like her. You didn't even want to meet her."

"I know..."

"So somehow you're twisting things up in your head. You're thinking that just because you like Jin and want to treat her well...that it somehow means you love your mother less."

I nodded. "Yeah, I think so."

"But that's not true. Do you know how proud your mom would be of you right now, Kim? Can you imagine how she'd be smiling to see that the daughter she raised is fixing this nice meal and using the good china and even putting flowers on the table? That would make her so happy!"

I considered this. "You know, I think you're right."

"Of course, I'm right."

Now I studied Nat for a long moment. "And when did you get so smart, Natalie McCabe?"

"Guess it was the school of hard knocks." She gave me a lopsided grin.

Then I hugged her again. "I'm so glad you're helping me tonight."

Then Nat said that she thought we should take a couple of minutes to pray, to ask God to put His blessing on the evening and to make sure that all went well. And that's just what we did.

And amazingly—or maybe not so amazingly when you consider our prayer—things did go well. The food came out just like the little old guy promised. Even my dad was impressed.

"This was an excellent dinner," he told me as we were finishing.

"Thanks." I grinned at him. "Natalie helped too."

"Not much," Nat said quickly. "I was just the cook's helper."

"How did you learn to cook like this?" Jin asked me.

I shrugged. "I guess I'm still learning. But my mom taught me a lot."

"I don't know how to cook," she admitted.

"Really?" Nat looked stunned. "Not at all?"

"Not at all. I eat my meals out or order food to bring home."

"Wow, that must be nice," Nat told her. I could tell that Nat was impressed with Jin. And I couldn't wait until Nat and I were alone and she could tell me what she really thought.

"We have a very light dessert," I announced, "since I know from last night that Jin doesn't care much for sweets."

"And we'll be serving that in the living room," Nat added. "Actually, I'll be serving it." She looked directly at me. "You three can go and make yourselves comfortable."

I kind of blinked. "Well, okay."

Then Nat took orders for coffee and tea, and I asked her if she was sure she wanted to do this on her own, and she insisted.

"You have a lovely home," Jin said as Dad and I walked her into the living room.

"Thank you," my dad told her. "We enjoy it."

"It is so much larger than my apartment in Puson. But large places are very expensive in the city. And besides, I am only one person, and I am not even home very much." She picked up the leather briefcase that was sitting on the hall tree. "I want to give you some photographs, Kim."

So we sat on the couch and looked at old pictures of some very formal-looking Korean people. It was hard to imagine that these strangers were actually my relatives. Then finally she showed me an old black-and-white photo of a girl about my age.

"She looks like Kim," my dad said.

"My mother."

I studied the photo, the serious eyes, small chin, broad cheekbones. "She does look a little like me."

"She was considered very beautiful," Jin told me. "Many men wanted to marry her. And her parents were wealthy, so they could be choosy."

"Did she love her husband?" I asked.

"I think she did. Although they had been married for many years by the time I was born. It is possible they were simply accustomed to each other. It was not the sort of thing they spoke of."

"Here we go," Nat said as she carried in a tray with four neatly arranged bowls of raspberry sorbet, adorned with the mint leaves we'd picked earlier from my mom's little herb garden outside the kitchen. "I'll be right back with coffee and tea."

"Does this mean we have to give you a tip?" my dad teased.

Soon we were all eating dessert, examining the photos, and visiting like we'd known each other for years.

"It is so wonderful to finally see you," Jin said to me as we put the photos away. "To see what a fine young woman you have grown to be."

"And she plays the violin beautifully," Natalie said suddenly. "You should hear her."

"I would love to hear," said Jin. "Is it too much to ask?"

"Come on, Kim," my dad urged.

So off I went to get my violin. Fortunately, it was already tuned. I warmed up a bit, then played a couple of classical pieces. I was so caught up in my playing that I wasn't paying much attention to my audience. But when I finished, Jin was crying.

"I am so proud of you," she said to me. Then she turned to my dad. "You and your wife are to be praised. You have done a beautiful job."

My dad looked a little misty eyed just then. He paused, looking at me, then looking back to Jin. "It was as if we were given this young tender shoot. We weren't even quite sure what we were supposed to do with her. But we loved and nurtured her the best we could, and she thrived and grew—" he shook his head now, almost as if in disbelief—"and blossomed into this amazing young woman we see today."

I giggled. "My head is going to be so big that I won't be able to get through the doorway."

Jin frowned and my dad explained the corny metaphor, which made her laugh.

"But seriously," I said, still standing, "God deserves some credit too." And then, quite out of the blue, I began to talk about how lost I'd felt just a few years ago. I told about how I started this journey, searching for who I was. First thinking that I needed to find my ancestral roots but coming up empty. Then attempting to find myself in Buddhism but only feeling more lost.

"It wasn't until I gave my heart to Jesus that life started to really make sense," I told Jin. "And I thank God I figured that out when I did." I shook my head. "I never would've survived losing Mom without that."

Jin seemed to be considering this.

"And I watched Kim going through all this," Nat added. "I can tell you that this girl is a changed person."

"So while my parents deserve a ton of credit for raising me right," I said, smiling at Dad, "and while Jin can claim a connection to me through DNA, it's because of God that I am who I am. And I'm really thankful for that."

We talked some more after that. Mostly Nat and I

asked Jin questions about Korea and the places she'd traveled. Nat even asked her about where she shopped for clothes.

"You're so stylish," Nat said.

Jin looked slightly embarrassed. "To use an American term, my girlfriend says that I am a shopaholic." She held her hand over her mouth. "And I'm afraid it is true."

"Well, I'd sure love to go shopping with you," Nat said.

I nodded. "Yes. Nat wishes she could be a shopaholic too."

We all laughed.

Finally it was getting late. "I have an early morning flight," Jin told us. "It is probably time for me to go."

"I can drive you back to the hotel," I offered. Dad and I had already prearranged this idea as a way for me to have the last few minutes with Jin.

"And I'm on clean-up crew," my dad said.

"I'll help," offered Nat.

So they told Jin good-bye, and I drove her back downtown in my Jeep.

"Kim," she said as I pulled up to her hotel, "you are an impressive girl. You are beautiful and smart. You play the violin and cook. And you can even drive!"

I laughed.

"No, I'm serious," she said. "I cannot cook or drive."

"You don't drive?" I said, amazed.

She shook her head. "No. In the city, there is no place for a car. I never even learned to drive."

I patted the steering wheel of my Jeep. "I love driving. And I love my Jeep. I call her Daisy."

Jin laughed. "A Jeep called Daisy!"

"And can I tell you a secret?"

Her eyes lit up. "Yes! Yes! Please, do. I can be trusted."

So I told her about the advice column in the paper. "It's called Just Ask Jamie," I said. "And about twenty other newspapers have syndicated it."

She nodded. "You will be rich."

I laughed. "Well, not rich. But it is fun."

"Will you send me copies of this column? This Just Ask Jamie?"

"For sure."

"I am going to look into your God, Kim. And your Jesus."

"Really?"

She nodded firmly. "Yes. I can see He has done a much better job with you than I did with my life when I was your age."

I didn't say anything.

"But I wouldn't change it." She smiled now. "Because then you wouldn't be here, would you?"

"God really does bring good things out of bad."

"I think you are right." She turned to the door. "Now how do you open this?"

So I hopped out, went around, and opened her door. "Like this."

She laughed. "You are very talented."

"May I hug you?" I asked her now, unsure as to what she'd think of this request.

"Oh, please. Please do!"

And so we hugged. And when we let go, we were both crying.

"I am so glad to know you," she told me. "But I do not know how to be a mother, Kim."

I nodded. "I already had a mother. And to be honest, you don't seem old enough to be my mother. I think I'd rather think of you like a sister." I smiled at her. "I never had a sister."

"Oh, that is perfect!" She clapped her hands. "And now you must promise to come to Puson sometime. You must come and see where your roots were first planted. Before your shoot was carried over to this country."

"I would love that."

Then we hugged again.

And now I'm thinking that I really would like to go to Korea. I'd like to see where Jin lives and works and who her friends are. Oh, I don't think it'll happen anytime soon. But maybe someday. In the meantime, I will continue getting to know Jin—not as a mother, but as a sister. I can deal with that.

Dear Jamie,

My sister is driving me crazy. She's a freshman and I'm a junior, and it's like she never lets up. Everything I have, she wants. She borrows stuff all the time without asking. She says things to get me in trouble with my parents. She flirts with my boyfriend. And then she wants me to give her and her friends rides everywhere. She is making my life perfectly miserable. Short of killing her, what do you think I should do?

Sister Hater

Dear SH,

I don't think you really hate your younger sister. But I do think she's getting to you. Maybe you need to set some boundaries. Let her know what's okay and what's not. If she steps over the line, like taking your stuff, then ask your parents to get involved. I suspect that she just admires you, wants to be like you, and is trying to get your attention. Maybe if you let her know that you actually like her, she'll let up a little.

Just Jamie

Eighteen

Monday, April 2

Today was the first day back at school after spring break. Spring break was pretty uneventful, but I didn't really care. It was kind of nice to just hang out. Nat and I hung around town and did some pretty ordinary things, and as a result, I'm feeling kind of relaxed and refreshed and ready to hit the books again.

Jin and I have been keeping up a fairly steady e-mail correspondence. As promised, I sent her some copies of my column, and she was impressed. She has a friend who's an editor at a newspaper and is actually going to ask him about syndicating it. That would be my first foreign syndication. And I'm pretty sure it's a long shot. But it's fun to think about anyway.

I've had several disturbing e-mails from my cousin Maya during the past couple of weeks. It sounds like her mom is really going off the deep end. Maya says that sometimes Shannon leaves home for several days at a time, then she comes back like nothing's wrong. But the e-mail I got today was really unsettling. So much so that I'm asking Dad to take action. Maya needs help.

> hi kim. sorry to bug you so much, but i don't know what to do. don't know who to talk to. shannon's been awol 5 days this time. i know she's probably ok, but sometimes i think maybe she's dead. our bills r not paid. people keep calling asking where is she? and when money is coming? finally i took phone off hook. can't take it. if you call me, it will just ring and ring. not that you'd call. i do appreciate your emails. i have to email from my friend's house now since our internet is cut off. if i knew how to reach my dad, i would ask him to help. my friend says i should go to authorities, but that's scary. who knows where i'd end up? some people don't think 16 is old enough to take care of yourself. unfortunately i know better. i think i'll get a job so at least I have money for food. but that means no more school. ha-school is a joke anyway. thanks for listening. your cuz, maya.

Dad frowns as he reads the e-mail I printed out for him.

"Sorry to dump on you," I say quickly. "And as soon

as you get home from work. But I'm worried about Maya."

He nods and sits down at his desk. "You should be."

"She sounds so desperate. So hopeless."

"This would break your mother's heart, Kim."

"I know, Dad. Is there some way we can help her?"

"She seems to be asking for help..."

"In her own way, I think she's screaming for help. You remember how strong and independent she was when they were here? Could you imagine that girl asking anyone to help her?"

He shakes his head as he studies the e-mail. "I think you're right about your aunt, Kim."

"You mean the drug thing?"

He nods.

"Maya's the one who told me that. I guess I wasn't so sure at first. I mean, it just seemed weird. You think about kids doing drugs...not grown-ups, not parents."

"Grown-ups can be just as messed up as kids."

"I'm amazed that Maya's not more messed up."

"But for how long?" He slides the e-mail back to me. "What do you want to do, Kim?"

"Why are you asking me?"

"Because if you're thinking what I'm thinking, it'll be mostly up to you."

"Are you thinking about asking Maya to come here?"

"Are you?"

I nod. "You'd be willing to take her in?"

"Would you?"

I think hard about this. "I know she can be a pain, Dad. But if we established some rules, right from the start, maybe it could work."

"You'd be the one stuck with her for the most part, Kim. Of course, we have no idea how long she'd be here. She might get sick of us after two days."

I look at her e-mail again. "It does seem like a real cry for help."

"Well, it looks like you can't call her. Why don't you e-mail her back and see how she feels about coming out for a visit. She may say to forget it."

"Yeah. I guess that wouldn't surprise me much."

"Tell her we'll buy her a ticket," he says as he turns on his computer.

"Thanks, Dad!" I hug him, then go back to my room and immediately e-mail her.

Dear Maya,

It sounds like Shannon is really having some big problems. My dad and I discussed this whole thing, and we both agree that it might be good to have you come out and stay with us for a while. Just for a break, you know. It might give you time to figure some things out. You are our family, Maya, and we care about you. My dad will buy your plane ticket. Just let us know if you're interested, and he will set it all up.

Take care,

Kim

Friday, April 6

Today was a long day. I went to the Paradiso right after school and worked until closing. And, okay, it's a fun place to work. But by the time I got home, I was exhausted. Even so, I decided to check e-mail. I've been checking regularly, desperately hoping to hear back from Maya. I've been worried that no news might be bad news. And finally, tonight, there is an e-mail!

> hi kim. i meant to email you sooner. but things got crazy. just when i thought i cud breathe again, because shannon came home late monday night, with money and acting like everything was groovy again, then suddenly life fell totally apart. let me explain. shannon was all sorry for being gone so long. she said it was "business." yeah, right. but since she had money, i thought maybe we were going to be ok. then yesterday afternoon, the police show up. ok, i got so scared that i just hid. there's a spot in the attic no one knows about but me. I could hear lots of noise and i know they were doing a big search in our house. for drugs, i'm sure. i could hear shannon screaming at the cops. but i cudn't go down there. i knew they would take me too. finally it got quiet. shannon was gone. i think she was arrested. probably a possession charge. or maybe dealing. i always knew this wud happen, but now that it's here, i am freaking. if your dad really

means it i wud like to come stay with you.

maybe just until i know what to do, or maybe get hold of my dad. i'm hiding out at home and a friend's house. our phone is off now. here's my friend's phone number (1-612-555-7912) her name is campbell. she will take my messages. i want out of here. the sooner the better. thanks.

maya

My dad was awake when I got home, but I'm not so sure now. I tiptoe past his bedroom and see a slat of light beneath the door. I tap lightly. "Dad?"

"Come in."

I see him sitting up in bed, with a reading light on. He's got a mystery propped up in front of him. Such a cozy scene.

"I hate to disturb you."

"You're not disturbing me, Kim. What is it?"

So I tell him about Maya, spilling her story in one great long run-on sentence.

"Oh dear." He sits up straighter.

"Do you know what to do? I mean, to handle this? Do we have to let anyone know or anything?"

He frowns. "I'm not sure. But I can find out in the morning. Do you think she'll be okay for the night?"

"I think so. She just sounds extremely scared."

"Well, I'll be on it first thing in the morning, Kim. Don't worry. We'll figure this out."

"Thanks, Dad. I hope it's not a mistake."

He smiles. "All we can do is what we think is best."

"Let God take care of the rest?"

"You sound like your mother, Kim."

"Good."

"Good night," he says. "Don't let worries about Maya keep you awake, sweetheart."

"I'm going to pray my worries away, Dad."

He nods. "Yep, just like your mom."

Sunday, April 8

Dad, true to his word, figured out a way to safely and legally get Maya out here. She arrived this afternoon and, to our surprise and relief, acted like a completely different person. Okay, she's pretty gloomy. But at least she's not picking fights with anyone. Not yet anyway.

"Part of the agreement," my dad informed her on the way home from the airport, "is to get you enrolled in school." He cleared his throat. "Will that be a problem for you, Maya?"

"No."

"Kim has offered to take you with her tomorrow. She'll show you what to do and who to talk to."

"Okay."

"Even though the year's mostly over," I said, "if you decide to stay here longer, like next year, well, it would be good to get started this year."

"Next year?" Her dark brows arched now.

"Oh, we don't really know about that," my dad said

quickly. "I think this will be a one-day-at-a-time sort of thing."

"Oh..." Maya seemed to relax a bit. And I decided I better not push things with this girl.

We showed Maya her room, the same one that Nat used last year. And she seemed to think it would be okay.

"You didn't bring much," I mentioned when I realized she only had two bags.

"I travel light."

"Well, if you need anything...I mean, if you forgot something, just ask."

"Thanks."

I noticed the dark circles beneath her eyes now. "You look tired, Maya. Feel free to rest or whatever."

"I am tired. I haven't really slept too well, you know, lately."

I nodded. "I understand."

So she slept most of the afternoon. But I stuck around the house just in case she woke up and wanted to talk. Then we ordered pizza for dinner, eating it in front of the TV since there was an action movie Dad wanted to see. But it seemed a good way to just chill with Maya. Let her adjust to us.

Then before she went to bed, she thanked me again. "I really don't know where I'd be..." she sighed, "if you guys hadn't helped me. I do appreciate it."

I wanted to hug her, but I sensed that would be stepping over some invisible line. "I'm glad you came," I said instead. "I'd like to get to know you better." Then I told her what time we'd be leaving for school, and I could tell she was a little shocked. But she didn't say anything negative. It gives me hope.

Friday, April 13

Okay, I can't say this has been the easiest week of my life. But I guess it could've gone worse. On the upside, Maya has decided she likes some of my friends. Particularly Marissa. It figures. And Maya likes the Paradiso. I think she also likes Chloe, Allie, and Laura who are here for a few days for a brief break from their tour. Maybe it's because, like her dad, they are musicians. But Maya didn't want me to tell anyone who her dad is. Not that too many of my friends would know or care, but some would.

"Why not?" I asked her.

"I don't want people to like me because of my dad."

I nodded. "Yeah, that makes sense."

"If someone doesn't like me, I want to know up front. I don't want them pretending, you know."

Now the downside of this first week with Maya is just Maya. Although I'm sure she's trying to be nice, she has this very edgy side to her. Since she's a vegan, she gets down on anyone who eats meat or any animal by-product, even milk or cheese. She and Nat got into it over this yesterday. Although, I have to give Nat credit, she's being a lot more patient than she might've been a year ago. Mostly she was just trying to make Maya look at the bigger picture.

"If you really love animals," Nat said on the way home from school yesterday, "I'd think you'd be worried about all the cows, pigs, chickens, and whatever that are being raised around the country."

"I am worried. That's why I'm vegan."

"But think about it," Nat continued. "What if everyone suddenly became a vegan?"

"That'd be great."

"But what would happen to all the farm animals?"

"They'd be happy."

"No." Nat shook her head. "They'd be dead."

Maya didn't say anything. But I got it.

"That's right," I chimed in. "There would be no need for them anymore. And what farmer is going to pay good money to feed and care for animals that have no value?"

"Yep," said Nat. "It's all about the bottom line. All those animals would probably be killed instantly. It would be a great big cow, pig, and chicken holocaust."

"Talk about sad." I shook my head.

Okay, Maya looked like she was fuming. And I did feel a little bad, like we were ganging up on her. But we were just being honest.

"I can understand how you feel," I finally said, the guilt getting to me. "I actually became a vegetarian once."

"Once?"

"Well, it didn't last more than a couple of weeks," I admitted. "But I'd seen a TV news show about how beef is processed." I made a face. "Eeeuw! It was so gross. And I felt so sorry for the cattle being slaughtered that I totally quit eating meat."

"Why'd you go back to it?"

"I'm not sure... I guess I wasn't convinced that my not eating it would do any good."

"Well, maybe it does me some good," Maya said.

"I can respect that," I told her.

"Me too," said Nat.

Of course, then Nat got into it with Maya again today. This time over leather. Nat had gotten a new purse that Maya pointed out was made of "dead cow." Oh well.

Dear Jamie,

How old do you think is old enough to date? I know some girls who've been dating since middle school. Not that I think that's so good. There are three girls in my family, and my parents said no dating until we're eighteen. And they enforced this rule with my older sister, but then she went to college last fall, and I happen to know she's been sleeping with half the guys she dates. I'm the middle daughter and I just turned sixteen, and I don't think it's fair to wait until I'm eighteen. What do you think?

Ready to Date

Dear Ready,

I think you need to discuss this with your parents. But first of all, you might want to make a list of all the reasons why you think you're old enough to date. Parents like that sort of thing. And in all fairness, you should list the reasons you think you might not be old enough as well. See how these lists weigh against each other. Then in a mature fashion, present your concerns to your parents. Try to discuss the pros and cons without turning it into a battlefield. Fighting will only show them how juvenile you are. Then hope for the best.

Just Jamie

Nineteen

Thursday, April 26

Okay, I guess I know how it feels to be a mother. Sort of. I'm sure I've mentioned before in my diary that Maya is a very beautiful girl. She's biracial and very exotic looking. She has these intense brown eyes, bronze skin, and soft, dark curly hair that goes past her shoulders. And even though she's an earth muffin who practically lives in overalls, tie-dye, and Birkenstocks, she's managed to catch the eyes of a few males at our school.

It figures that Spencer would be one of them. Now, I will give Spencer this much credit—I think he has quit using drugs. But he still drinks and smokes and picks on Christians. Although, for as much as he picks on Christians, he doesn't mind hanging with them. Our theory is that he's a Christian wannabe, but too afraid to lose his bad boy image. Anyway, Cesar and Jake refuse to give up on their old buddy, and I gotta admit that I think it's kind of cool.

But when Spencer invited Maya to prom? Well, I had to wonder what was up with that. Fortunately, Maya turned him down. She said she thought prom sounded juvenile. But then Spencer agreed, saying he only asked because she was new at school and he thought it was something she'd be into. And everything would've been just fine, but then Spencer asked her to go out with him. And she agreed!

Okay, my first instinct was to put my foot down. To tell her that she couldn't go out with a guy like that. Then I had to realize how ridiculous that would sound and how it would probably just make her want to go out with him even more. So I actually prayed about the whole thing. And here's what I did. I decided to just be honest, to warn her, and to let her know I cared about her.

"You'll obviously make up your own mind about this," I said finally, after I'd shared my concerns. "And I have to admit that Spencer has changed some, but he does have a drug past, and I know how you feel about that."

She nodded, as if taking this in. "Well, you could be right. But since I told him I'd go out, I guess it can't hurt. And if it makes you feel any better, I've been in some pretty rough situations in the past. I know how to take care of myself. So you don't need to worry."

And somehow I believed her. Just the same, I told

Dad what was up before I went to bed tonight. And he just laughed.

"I know you really care about her," he told me. "But as long as Maya abides by our simple rules, which she appears to be doing, we can't really dictate to her who she can or cannot date. Can we?"

"No. I just wanted to let you know."

He hugged me. "You're going to be a good mom someday, Kim."

"Just not with Maya?"

"I think it's a little too late for that. Maya needs a good, wise friend more than a teenage 'mom' right now."

"I think you're right."

"And if anyone needs to play the parent card," he winked, "I guess it should be me."

And I guess he's right. Besides, it takes the pressure off me. And like Maya insinuated, if anyone can take care of herself, she can.

Sunday, April 29

Today is the anniversary of Mom's death. I didn't tell anyone, but it's like I could feel the memory of it hovering around me all day. I suspect my dad thought about this too. But neither of us mentioned it. I think I was afraid that if I said something, it would just make him feel worse. Maybe he was thinking the same about me.

The good news is that I do feel better than I felt last year at this time. I guess these things really do get better with time. Even so, it still hurts.

Finally, I pulled out the letter she wrote me shortly before her death. I'm afraid I'm going to wear it out since I read it so much during those first few months. But it had been a while, and I decided that it was appropriate to read it on the anniversary of her death. And even though it made me cry, they were good tears. And it was good to be reminded of her—I never want to forget her.

Dear Kim,

If you are reading this letter, I must be gone. To say that I know how you feel is rather presumptuous on my part, but I do remember how I felt when I lost my mother so many years ago. It's something you never forget. And although I am tired and my body is failing me now, I would give anything to stay here with you—to watch you graduate from high school (with honors!) and then college (with even more honors!) and to see you launched into some impressive career (probably with even more honors!) and then one day to see you walk down the aisle with your true love and then later on to bounce a grandbaby on my knee. Oh, what I would give to be there with you for all those events.

Sweet Kim, you have been the most

precious gift in my life. When I realized that I was unable to bear children, I believed that God had another plan. And He did! I will never forget the day we picked you up at the orphanage in Seoul. You were only four months old, but you were already sitting up—and those big dark eyes were so alert, so wise! We knew from the start that you were a special child. I instantly fell in love with you, sweetheart. And my love for you has only grown over the years.

I'm sorry that I can't physically be with you anymore. But I have this deep sense, this blessed assurance, that I'll be able to check in on you from time to time—like when you graduate or marry or have children... Goodness, it wouldn't be heaven if I were cut off from my two loved ones permanently, now would it? So please know that although I am away, I am still here. My love for you will go on forever. And eventually we will all be together again. I believe that with my whole heart. In the meantime, we will just do our best, won't we? And knowing you, my Kim, you will do better than your best—you always do.

Now here is my final wish for you, sweetheart. It's something I've never really put into words but have always wanted to say: Take time to breathe, to feel the sun on your head, to smell the roses, and to laugh. You've always been a serious girl, but don't forget to have fun, to appreciate the goodness all around you, and to hear the birds singing in the trees. Those are all God's gifts to you, and I want you to enjoy them—and to enjoy the wonderful life that is stretched out before you! And when you do those things, my sweet daughter, remember me!

Love always and forever,

Mom

Sunday, May 6

Maya has been here almost a month now, and I'm amazed at how well it's going. Oh, she's still Maya with all her funny hang-ups and California ways. But I can tell that she's softening up some too. She actually goes to youth group with me, and she even asks some pretty intelligent questions. Well, along with some slightly embarrassing ones. Like the time she really got into the whole Adam and Eve thing by asking how their kids reproduced without committing incest if there weren't any other people around. Although, I must say, Josh handled it quite well.

And today, for the first time, she went to church with me. And she even said that she agreed with "some of the sermon." I told her I thought she was a searcher. And she agreed. Okay, I didn't tell her that I'm pretty sure she's searching for God. But I think it's true. And as much as I want her to find Him, I'm not pushing her. However, I am praying.

She's had a few short yet emotional conversations with her mom. It sounds like Shannon's going to be locked up for some time. Maya was right about the charges (possession and selling narcotics as well as a few other things), and as a result, Shannon's bail is set pretty high, and no one has stepped up to fork over the cash yet. I know we're not going to do it. Dad said that as much as he cares about Shannon, he isn't willing to risk my college savings for her.

Maya says their house has been refinanced so many times that the bank has probably already taken possession. I'm thinking it might be for the best for Shannon to spend some time in jail. It might give her time to think about stuff and maybe even get clean. Although I've heard that some people can still get drugs while incarcerated.

Anyway, it looks like Maya's going to be here for a while. And she's already signed up to take some remedial summer classes so she can enter school as a junior in the fall. Lucky for her, she's really smart, and despite her raggedy homeschool records, she's quickly getting up to speed. It's encouraging to see her determination. It's also fun to see that she has something she really loves doing: art. And it turns out she's quite an artist. She's already hooked up with the art department and gotten herself on the waiting list for a summer art program where kids get to paint murals on public buildings. I'm hoping and praying that she'll get to do it. I even told her a little about Matt and his interest in art and some of the things he got to do.

"Matt, your boyfriend?" she asks quickly.

"I'm surprised you even remember him."

"I met him at the funeral." She grins. "I thought he was pretty cute. Why'd you guys break up anyway?"

I give her the short version.

"Too bad," she says.

"No, actually it was good. I was ready to move on by then."

And as I record this in my diary, I'm amazed that I no longer feel the slightest twinge of regret over Matt. It's like that was then and this is now, and I'm so over him. And I realize that although I did care about him and I really liked him, he was never the love of my life. I was never really in love—not in that big way, the way I hope to be someday when the timing is right and the guy is Mr. Right. This thought makes me feel happy inside.

Monday, May 14

Yesterday was Mother's Day. And, okay, it wasn't easy. Dad and I had already decided to go put flowers on Mom's grave to honor her. We invited Maya to come, but she said she had homework, plus she thought it would be better if just the two of us went. And I really respect her for that. Dad took a dozen red roses, which seemed appropriate. And I took a small bouquet from the little flower bed I've been taking care of in front of our house. I still remember when Mom and I planted flowers there last year. It looks even better this year. I think she'd like that.

"We're getting past this, Kimmy," my dad said as we got back into the car.

"I know," I told him. Even so, there was a lump in my throat.

He reached over and squeezed my arm. "But we'll never forget her."

I nodded. A single tear streaked down my cheek.

Saturday, June 2

I graduated from high school last night. It's over and done with and like so yesterday now, but it was so cool. No one seemed terribly surprised when I was named as valedictorian. Although I think I was. I mean, I knew it was fairly likely and I was hoping for it, but like so many other things in life, you just never really know until it happens. So I guess I was relieved.

I sweated over my speech, writing and rewriting it until it sounded phony even to me. Finally, I just tossed it and decided to wing it. Of course, as the moment drew closer and I could see the packed-out auditorium, I realized that I would soon be in the spotlight, and well, I almost had a full-blown panic attack. "Just breathe," I told myself as my heart threatened to leap from my chest. Finally, I prayed. "God, give me the words. Please, give me the words that will encourage everyone—mostly the kids in my class. Give me the words."

And, okay, I can't remember exactly what I said since I was so scared, but I'll do my best to put it down here.

"Friends, family, faculty, and fellow graduates," I began with confidence. Sure, that part came easy since I'd written it down at least a dozen times. "I'm really honored to be standing before you tonight."

Then I paused and really looked out over the sea of faces from my class looking up at me. "And one of the reasons I'm so honored is because I know you guys. I've gone to school with some of you for twelve years or more. And over the years I've come to really love and respect and care about you."

I paused again. "Okay, some of you who know me might be thinking that I haven't always been like that. And I have to admit it's true. There have been times when I didn't really want to know you, times when I made quick judgments about you, or times when I took you for granted."

I slowly shook my head. "And I am so sorry for that now. In the past year, I've come to realize how much each and every one of you has to offer. And I've really started to appreciate all of you. And now that it's time to say good-bye, I see how unique and interesting and fun you guys are. And I'm starting to understand how much I'm going to miss you. And that makes me sad. Really sad."

I think my voice even cracked about then. "But it's a

good kind of sadness, a sadness that's the by-product of loving people, caring about them so much that you value them and realize that their absence will leave a small hole in your life. But it's a good hole."

I smiled then. "It's like the way that I feel when I remember my mom." I paused again, almost unsure of where I was going with all this. "But this is a time of looking forward," I said quickly. "A time of great expectations, a time for embarking on new adventures, a time of stepping into a new life. And if there is one bit of encouragement that I can leave with you tonight, this would be it: Don't do it alone. Do not go by yourself. God designed us to need each other. He made us with the ability to give and receive."

I looked around the room. "So as you go through life, take the hand of someone and let someone take you by the hand. Be a friend and allow yourself to be befriended. Because when it's all said and done, when we've finished our adventures, after we've lived our lives—it won't be our accomplishments or the things we've acquired that we'll remember. It will be the people, our dear friends and loved ones, who will stand out in our memories.

"So, I thank you guys," I said finally. "Thank you for being a part of my life, for being a part of my memories. God bless all of you!"

And then I waved good-bye and stepped away from the podium. Tears blurred my eyes as I returned to my seat, and I got this very distinct feeling that my mom was watching this whole thing—that she was up there in heaven just clapping and cheering for me. And I felt pretty sure that I'd made her proud, and God willing, I would continue to make her proud.

Then we all took turns marching up to the stage where we received our diplomas and handshakes, and to my personal relief, Spencer didn't turn around and moon the spectators like he'd threatened to do earlier this week.

"That was a great speech," Nat told me after the ceremony finally ended and a few of us gathered in a circle to congratulate each other.

"Yeah," said Chloe. "Even though I graduated early, I still felt like it was for me too."

"What you said about needing friends was awesome," said Cesar.

"So true," echoed Allie. "We'd be lost without friends."

Then about a dozen of us huddled together in a somewhat sloppy group hug before we all threw our graduation caps up into the air and shouted out, "God bless the class of 2006!"

And for the most part, I think that God has already blessed us. Oh, I know that some kids, especially ones like Spencer and Marissa, are still a little confused about life and God and things that really matter. But I also think some important seeds have been planted during the past few years. And I have no doubt that those seeds will start to sprout when the timing is right.

Because one thing I know for sure—God is the master of the impossible. He can do anything! And as I prepare for the next stage of my life, I look forward with happy anticipation to whatever comes next! It's gotta be good!

Reader's Guide

1. Kim underwent something of a spiritual awakening in *Falling Up* (the previous book). How do you think that impacted her life in this story?

2. To start out, Natalie is determined to marry Ben and keep her baby, but Kim is feeling pretty freaked. How would you handle this if you were Nat's best friend?

3. There are early signs of trouble in Nat and Ben's marriage. Why do you think they were having such a struggle? What could they have done differently?

4. Do you think Kim was right to tell Josh and Caitlin about what was going on with Nat and Ben? Or was it just gossip? Explain.

5. How do you think Natalie felt after realizing that her marriage wasn't going to work? What would you have said to her if you were her friend?

6. Kim was strongly supportive of adoption for Nat's baby. How do you feel about this? Is adoption always the best option? Why or why not?

7. Why do you think Nat's mom was being so negative and unsupportive? How did you feel about the role she played in her daughter's life?

8. Were you surprised by Kim's reaction to the first communication she received from her birth mother? How would you feel if you were Kim?

9. Do you think it was important for Kim to actually meet her birth mother? Why or why not?

10. Kim's graduation speech focused on how vital friends were in her life. Do you agree with that about your own life? Why or why not?

11. Kim felt confident about her future. Why do you think that is? How do you feel about your own future? Explain.

Diary of a Teenage Girl Series

Caitlin

Diaries Are a Girl's Best Friend

DIARY OF A TEENAGE GIRL, Caitlin book one
Follow sixteen-year-old Caitlin O'Conner as she makes her way through life—surviving a challenging home life, school pressures, an identity crisis, and the uncertainties of "true love." You'll cry with Caitlin as she experiences heartache, and cheer for her as she encounters a new reality in her life: God. See how rejection by one group can—incredibly—sometimes lead you to discover who you really are.

IT'S MY LIFE, Caitlin book two
Caitlin faces new trials as she strives to maintain the recent commitments she's made to God. Torn between new spiritual directions and loyalty to Beanie, her pregnant best friend, Caitlin searches out her personal values on friendship, dating, life goals, and family.

WHO I AM, Caitlin book three
As a high school senior, Caitlin's relationship with Josh takes on a serious tone via e-mail—threatening her commitment to "kiss dating good-bye." When Beanie begins dating an African American, Caitlin's concern over dating seems to be misread as racism. One thing is obvious: God is at work through this dynamic girl in very real but puzzling ways, and a soul-stretching time of racial reconciliation at school and within her church helps her discover God's will as never before.

ON MY OWN, Caitlin book four
An avalanche of emotion hits Caitlin as she lands at college and begins to realize she's not in high school anymore. Buried in coursework and far from her best friend, Beanie, Caitlin must cope with her new roommate's bad attitude, manic music, and sleazy social life. Should she have chosen a Bible college like Josh? Maybe…but how to survive the year ahead is the big question right now!

I DO, Caitlin book five
Caitlin, now 21 and in her senior year of college, accepts Josh Miller's proposal for marriage. But Caitlin soon discovers there's a lot more to getting married than just saying "I do." Between her mother, mother-in-law to be, and her old buddies, Caitlin's life never seems to run smoothly. As a result, the journey to her wedding is full of twists and turns where God touches many lives, including her own.

Log on to www.DOATG.com

Diary of a Teenage Girl Series

Chloe

MY NAME IS CHLOE, Chloe book one

Chloe Miller, Josh's younger sister, is a free spirit with dramatic clothes and hair. She struggles with her identity, classmates, parents, boys, and whether or not God is for real. But this unconventional high school freshman definitely doesn't hold back when she meets Him in a big, personal way. Chloe expresses God's love and grace through the girl band, Redemption, that she forms, and continues to show the world she's not willing to conform to anyone else's image of who or what she should be. Except God's, that is.

SOLD OUT, Chloe book two

Chloe and her fellow band members must sort out their lives as they become a hit in the local community. And after a talent scout from Nashville discovers the trio, all too soon their explosive musical ministry begins to encounter conflicts with family, so-called friends, and school. Exhilarated yet frustrated, Chloe puts her dream in God's hands and prays for Him to work out the details.

ROAD TRIP, Chloe book three

After signing with a major record company, Redemption's dreams are coming true. Chloe, Allie, and Laura begin their concert tour with the good-looking guys in the band Iron Cross. But as soon as the glitz and glamour wear off, the girls find life on the road a little overwhelming. Even rock-solid Laura appears to be feeling the stress—and Chloe isn't quite sure how to confront her about the growing signs of drug addiction...

FACE THE MUSIC, Chloe book four

Redemption has made it to the bestseller chart, but what Chloe and the girls need most is some downtime to sift through the usual high school stress with grades, friends, guys, and the prom. Chloe struggles to recover from a serious crush on the band leader of Iron Cross. Then just as an unexpected romance catches Redemption by surprise, Caitlin O'Conner—whose relationship with Josh is taking on a new dimension—joins the tour as a chaperone. Chloe's wild ride only speeds up, and this one-of-a-kind musician faces the fact that life may never be normal again.

Log on to www.DOATG.com

When **life** asks you tough **questions**...

...we want to help provide good **answers.**

ALSO FROM MELODY CARLSON

Dark Blue: Color Me Lonely
Brutally ditched by her best friend, Kara feels totally abandoned until she discovers these dark blue days contain a life-changing secret. 1-57683-529-4

Deep Green: Color Me Jealous
Stuck in a twisted love triangle, Jordan feels absolutely green with envy until her former best friend, Kara, introduces her to someone even more important than Timothy. 1-57683-530-8

Torch Red: Color Me Torn
Zoë feels like the only virgin on Earth. But now that she's dating Justin Clark, that seems like it's about to change. Luckily, Zoë's friend Nate is there to try to save her from the biggest mistake of her life. 1-57683-531-6

Pitch Black: Color Me Lost
Following her friend's suicide, Morgan questions the meaning of life and death and God. As she struggles with her grief, Morgan must make her life's ultimate decision—before it's too late. 1-57683-532-4

Burnt Orange: Color Me Wasted
Amber Conrad has a problem. Her youth group friends Simi and Lisa won't get off her case about the drinking parties she's been going to. *Everyone does it. What's the big deal?* Will she be honest with herself and her friends before things really get out of control? 1-57683-533-2

Look for the TrueColors series at a Christian bookstore near you or order online at www.navpress.com.

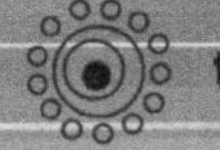

truecolors